Magic
of the
Bear

The Magic
of the Bear

Lenore Ashby

Illustrations by Brandy Collard

Grandma Chubby's Books
P.O. Box 902308 / Sandy, Utah 84090-2308

Published by
GRANDMA CHUBBY'S BOOKS
P.O. Box 902308
Sandy, Utah 84092

Cover illustration by Carol Erickson
Chapter illustrations by Brandy Collard
Permission to use pictographs and pictograph story from
Dover Publications Inc. N.Y.; *Indian Sign Language,* William Tomkins, 1969

Publisher's Cataloging-in-Publication
(Provided by Quality Books, Inc.)

Ashby, Lenore
    The Magic of the Bear / Lenore Ashby ; illustrations
by Brandy Collard. – 1st ed
    p. cm.
    SUMMARY: Two boys solve the mystery of a lost Ute
chief and discover the true meaning of friendship while
rescuing an albino bear cub and recovering the sacred bear
claw necklace.
    Audience: Ages 8-12.
    LCCN 2003090882
    ISBN: 0-9728535-0-2

    1. Ute Indians--Juvenile fiction. 2. Friendship--Juvenile
fiction. 3. Bears--Juvenile fiction. [1. Ute Indians--Fiction.
2. Friendship--Juvenile fiction. 3. Bears--Fiction.] I. Collard,
Brandy. II. Title

PZ7.A812Mag 2003   [Fic]
                      QB133-1206

Dedicated to

Hannah and Nicolas
Sara and Carter
Alex, Raistlin, Aurora and Grace
Cobi, Zoey and Bodi
and those yet to come.

The magic is for you!

Contents

CHAPTER 1

Bear Trouble!

O ne day I'm in school minding my own business, just like every other day of my life," Will muttered out loud. "The next thing I know, me and the whole family are on a wagon train crossing the Mississippi River and heading fer Indian country! Can you believe that, boy?" Tag did not respond. In fact, Tag, did not appear to be listening. He was busy trying to catch a butterfly on top of a flower that was at least six inches higher than his own head.

Will looked around at the immense, wild country he was standing in. The Rocky Mountains filled his vision to the east. Huge pine trees and acres of aspens covered the terrain. An eagle soared circles high in the air above him. He was a city boy come west. Sure they'd had a few horses and a cow out back, but compared to this place, where thousands of buffalo crossed the plains and cattle and sheep ran in huge herds, it was like they had never even seen real livestock before.

Will looked at Tag and let out a long sigh. He'd had lots of friends back in Boston and now his only friend was this ten inch, four-legged little puppy. Not that he wasn't thrilled to have his dog but oh, how his life had changed. He missed his friends and the good times they had together. Anything could happen to a person in this country. It wasn't civilized he'd heard tell. Why, one day you could be minding yer own business and the next thing you know, a pack a wild Indians would just as soon take yer scalp as look at you! Least ways, that's what his friends cautioned him as they waved good-bye. Amazingly, the wagon train had not had much interaction with Indians as they traveled West. But out here, in this huge wilderness it was another story. Will knew the Indians in the Utah Territory were nomadic. He and his family hadn't seen any yet but they had been well warned to keep their eyes peeled and be careful.

A sharp little bark snapped Will out of his thoughts. He felt a bead of sweat trickle down his spine beneath the thick cotton of his shirt. It was a warm day in May and he and Tag, had been exploring a large meadow. When tired of chasing the frisky little puppy, Will had decided to lie down and rest a bit. Looking up in response to Tag's bark, he saw the dog take off on a dead run, acting as though his very life depended on it.

"Hey, boy, where are you going?" Will called. He

jumped up and ran after the puppy.

"Grummpfh, grummpfh!" Surprised, Will stopped dead in his tracks, cocked his head sideways and listened intently.

"What in tarnation is that strange noise?" he whispered. Puzzled, he started to look around the meadow. Tag suddenly began barking furiously. "Quiet boy!" Will said a little bit anxiously.

Will dropped down to his hands and knees and began parting the tall grass. If something was out there he wanted to make sure he could see, but not be seen. He sucked in his breath and held it, hardly daring to breathe. Not twenty feet away, he spied a little white bear with startlingly pink eyes, rolling in the dirt, trying to scratch himself. Will had never been this close to a bear before. "He can't be very old," he whispered with surprise. "He isn't much bigger than you, Tag, and he doesn't seem to be afraid of either one of us!"

Will stared and was trying to decide what to do when Tag ran over to the bear and started barking again. The little cub rolled over and looked at Tag with a very puzzled expression. He reached his paw toward the puppy and started batting Tag around. Tag yipped with surprise and the cub cuffed him again. This time, Tag grabbed the bear's tail and gave it a good nip before jumping out of the path of the little cub's swinging paw.

"Hey you two, this isn't a boxing match!" Will laughed. All fear gone, he jumped up and grinned as he watched their rough play.

"Wait a minute! Where's your mother little bear?"

Will exclaimed, suddenly remembering that any kind of a baby is usually never very far from it's parent. Concerned, he looked around but the mother was nowhere to be seen. This could be very dangerous, he thought. Putting his hand over his eyes, Will scanned the area and tensed up as he strained to hear anything that might give him a clue that she was nearby.

"Yikes!" Will yelped as Tag ran right between his legs with the little bear in hot pursuit. Will tottered, lost his balance and fell hard on his rear end. He couldn't help himself and started to laugh at the antics of the two animals. "You come back, you little brats!" he called. Leaping to his feet he chased Tag and the little cub as they ran around the meadow. In the middle of all this frenzy, Will foolishly forgot about the mother bear.

It was useless trying to separate the two little animals. The fact that they were two different species didn't seem to matter at all to them. It wasn't long before Will got tired of chasing them. He stopped, wiped small beads of perspiration off his brow and took a deep breath. "Whew! I'm no match for those two," he said, and plopped down on the ground to rest. Amused, he watched the two little fur-balls leave him in the distance. This was more fun than he'd had in a long time.

Suddenly, Tag and the little bear disappeared from sight!

"Whaaat?" yelled Will. He jumped up and rubbed his eyes to make sure they weren't playing tricks on him. One second the two were running right in front of him, and the next they were gone.

Will sprang up and dashed to the spot where the two animals had disappeared. He looked around and saw that he was standing on the edge of a big ravine. Stooping down he cautiously leaned forward trying to see down the hill. It was steep and dropped off suddenly. On the very edge of the drop off, Will could see faint animal tracks. There was no mistaking the distinct marks left by the puppy and the little bear. But the tracks stopped right there. "Oh no!" Will whispered, "I'll bet they came too close to the edge and tumbled over!" By the looks of things he was almost positive this was the case.

Suddenly, Will felt himself starting to slide on the loose rock. Too late he realized he had gotten to close to the edge of the hill while concentrating on the animal tracks. "Tag, are you down there?" he yelled, at the same time grabbing frantically for anything to stop himself from falling. Clutching at nothing but empty air, he stumbled, tripped and, not being able to stop himself, began to slide down the steep incline. Rocks and dirt smeared his face, and he slammed his arm on a sharp root. "Ouch!" he yelped, as a hot twinge of pain traveled all the way down his arm to his fingers. But, just as quickly as the pain came, he ignored it. Right now, his only concern was finding Tag and that little bear.

"Ohhh", he moaned when he finally rolled to a stop near the bottom.

"Arrf, Arrf!" Will heard Tag wildly yapping at the bear and instantly, forgetting his own fall, jumped up to investigate. About ten feet away he found the little cub curled up into a ball and he was not moving. Without thinking, Will reached his hand out and gently touched the bear's small, round head. "Wow" he whispered, somewhat surprised. The cub's fur was not as soft as it looked. It felt wiry and coarse.

"Ooooh," groaned the cub.

Startled, Will moved his hand, but the cub ignored the human and continued to make funny little moaning sounds.

"He must have bumped his head," Will said thoughtfully. "He seems to be stunned. Come on, get up little bear! You gotta be all right!"

Tag started barking, and the little bear blinked his eyes. Slowly he rolled over and sat up. He paused, the pink eyes stared at Will. Startled, Will drew back. A shiver ran down his spine and a strange feeling came over him. It was almost as though he knew this bear. You're crazy, Will said to himself, this is an animal, not a person!

The moment ended as the little cub shook his head and started batting Tag around just as though nothing had happened. Will impatiently brushed his uneasy feelings away. He was just happy and relieved that the little bear had not been seriously injured.

"Crazy white boy," called a voice from behind him. Startled, Will stood up. Who in tarnation was that? Was he hearing things?

CHAPTER 2

Run for Your Life!

You come quick," the voice called again. Will turned around and stared at the tree line where the voice was coming from. His eyes widened with surprise when out of the trees stepped an Indian boy just about his own age. He was about the same height as Will but seemed to be a little bit thinner. His skin was a shiny coppery color and glistened in the sun. He had long black hair that hung below his shoulders and was pulled away from his eyes with a thick leather band. His eyes were deep black and had an urgency in them that pierced right through Will.

But Will had no time to stare, for suddenly the valley was filled with a huge roar. The noise was so loud it shook the trees. Spinning around, Will looked up to the top of the ravine and saw a huge black bear standing on her hind legs. For a second he wondered if this could be the cub's mother. But how on earth could a black bear have such a white baby? Will didn't have much time to try and figure this one out. The big bear's head was thrust toward the sky. Her mouth was wide open, showing rows of big, sharp teeth. Again, she let loose her fierce anger in another ear-deafening roar. There was no doubt about it, black or white, this was the cub's mother!

"You come now," came the urgent voice from among the tree line. Hesitating no longer, Will reached down and grabbed his trembling puppy. Just then the mother bear dropped to all fours and started making her way down the steep ravine. Will turned and ran as fast as he could.

Quickly, the Indian boy came out of his hiding place and ran to Will.

"White boy, you come!" he motioned.

Will held tightly onto Tag and together they followed the Indian. He glanced back just in time to see the baby bear run to meet his mother.

Will's feet pounded through the dirt and leaves of the forest. His breath came in ragged gasps and, every few minutes he nervously looked back to see if they were being followed. Through the trees and down paths the odd threesome raced. They ran and ran until they finally reached the river. Quickly, the Indian boy stepped into the shallow water and reached under some bushes that were hanging over the bank. A small, brown bark canoe floated out in front of him. He motioned for Will to get into the boat. Will hesitated for a fraction of a second. He'd never even met an Indian before, and now one wanted him to get into his canoe.

"ROOAARRR," came the distant voice of the mother bear. The loud sound vibrated the very ground they were standing on. It sounded as though she were right behind them, and Will could feel the noise travel all the way through his body. Any hesitation he had felt quickly disappeared and Will stepped from the bank into the middle of the little boat. The canoe rocked wildly back and forth, and he struggled to keep his balance. Steadying the craft, the Indian pushed the canoe out into the current and jumped in. He took his paddle and skillfully steered the boat into the middle of the river. Anxious, Will held Tag securely in his arms and then settled himself as far down into the bottom of the canoe as he could. His hand touched something soft and warm, and when he looked down he saw a stash of six dead rabbits underneath his palm. The Indian must have been hunting when he came across us, Will thought. He watched the boy with great interest and suddenly realized that he was actually with another person of his own age. When the boy turned and looked back, Will shyly pointed to himself and said, "I'm Will." He then pointed to the Indian and asked, "What is your name?"

The Indian smiled and replied, "Me Peteetneet (Paw-teet-neat), son of *Ute-ah* nation. Our people are *Wa-tue-weap-ah-Ute-ah.*"

"You speak English?" Will asked.

"Chief, my uncle. We talk with white trader many

time. Learn white man talk."

Will relaxed a little and watched the land move swiftly by as Peteetneet and the current carried them quickly downstream. Soon the river widened. The water became very calm, and Peteetneet steered the craft over to the other bank.

"We safe now. Get out and rest," said the Indian. The boat gently bumped into the soft mud on the bank and came to a stop. Peteetneet jumped out and held the craft steady while Will lifted Tag and himself over the edge onto the dry ground. Will stepped over to a large flat rock and sat down in relief. He realized his heart was still racing. Calm down! he told himself while trying to push aside his fears. Not only did you just escape from that crazy bear, but this Indian just saved your life!

Peteetneet walked over to the rock where Will was sitting. He sat cross-legged on the hard ground in front of him and looked firmly into Will's eyes.

"White boy do bad thing. Play with little bear is very dangerous. You very brave or maybe very crazy!" said Peteetneet.

Will got a sheepish look on his face. "I know it wasn't a very smart thing to do. The little white cub was so cute, and I thought the mother bear wasn't anywhere around."

"Mother bear always around. You lucky she not catch you at top of hill. Bear cannot run downhill very fast. Front legs too short."

Impulsively, Will reached deep into his pocket and pulled out his favorite marble. "You saved my life!" he said, "I want you to have this." It was made of glazed clay and painted to look like a moonstone. It was one of the few treasures he had been allowed to bring with him on his family's long trek west. Almost reverently, he placed the little round ball into Peteetneet's hand. "This is called a moonstone. It was my lucky taw. I always won with it."

Peteetneet looked at it with surprise and then with great pleasure.

"What is taw?" asked Peteetneet as he carefully turned the little ball in his hand.

"It's my shooter," said Will. "We play a game with lots of those balls. They're called marbles. We have to hit the marbles out of a ring in order to win. My taw is the marble I hit the other marbles out with. I always win with this one, and I want you to have it."

Peteetneet opened a little leather pouch hanging at the waistband of his breeches. He dropped the marble into the bag.

"My people play game like marble. We toss painted plum seeds into air and catch with bowl. Much fun. Someday I teach you. You teach me marble."

A grin of pure delight crossed Will's face. He hadn't played marbles for months now. For a split second his mind wandered back to the friends he had left in Boston. Every day after school they played marbles, and he had been the school champion. It all seemed so far away now. He smiled slightly. If his friends could see him right now they'd never believe it. With a sigh he jumped up and began searching among the leaves and rocks on the ground.

"Try to find me a few round rocks, and I'll teach you now," said Will. The rocky cliffs in this part of the land were made of red sandstone. Wind and water had broken down much of the terrain and near the river were many small, red and rounded sandstone pebbles. The boys searched carefully, and when they had found eight fairly round rocks, Will taught him how to play the game. Peteetneet flashed a big smile everytime his taw happened to hit one of the imitation marbles. Will soon forgot his earlier fears as he let himself become totally immersed in teaching his favorite game to this new friend.

"This isn't quite the same as when you have eight perfectly rounded marbles," Will said, "but I think this is one of the best games I've ever played!"

Soon, the afternoon began turning into evening. The sky became streaked with brilliant shades of red and gold.

"I've got to go!" Will said, as he watched the sun sinking into the west. "Will you meet me again?" he asked.

Peteetneet smiled, "I name you 'Little Bear', because you play with little cub who fall off mountain. We be friends from this day on."

Will nodded his head in happy agreement. "Tomorrow when the sun is straight up, meet me at the place in the river where the water falls over the cliff. I will wait at the bottom."

Peteetneet agreed. "Now I take you across river. Follow trail next to river, and it take you back to place I find you. Stay away from bear cub! You not so lucky next time!"

Peteetneet took Will across the river. They smiled at each other and parted. Will turned around once more to watch his new friend leave. "Who would have believed that a little bear could bring me such luck?" he said to Tag.

Will noticed the sun was now below the rim of the mountains. Ma and Pa would be very upset if he wasn't home before dark. "Come on, boy, we gotta git!" he said, and moving up the trail, he hurried towards home.

CHAPTER 3

Remembering Back—

When Will awoke, the sun had just started to shine through the small window in his room. Tag was on the floor rolling around and biting Will's boot. "Gimme that boot," Will said as he jumped out of bed and began a tug of war with Tag. "Sh-sh," he said, and he yanked the boot away. "I told Mama we were going early to try to find berries today. We don't want to wake anyone up." He had not told her about Peteetneet yet and he did not want to take the chance that she might not let him go to meet him.

Will pulled on his pants and quickly yanked his shirt over his tousled, blonde hair. He jerked up his suspenders and carelessly shoved the shirt down into his pants. With one hand he picked up his boots and socks and motioned Tag to follow him into the other room. On tiptoes, he opened the bread box and took out the hunk of bread and cooked potato his mother had left out for him. Very quietly he went out the front door into the clean air of the new morning.

"I better not forget the bucket," he said and walked towards the shed where the tack was kept. He picked up a wooden bucket and stuck his food down inside.

"Let's go, boy!" he called to Tag as he cheerfully headed towards the meadow. Will walked through some tall pines and felt a delicate little breeze brush across his face. "This is going to be a great day for us," he said.

Anticipation of meeting Peteetneet had his stomach doing flip-flops. It was more exciting than the day his Pa came home with Will's new little puppy. That day had meant a lot to Will because he finally had a friend to keep him company. Neighbors here were few and far between and it wasn't often he and his family had visitors.

"Two months ago, Tag, I never would have believed I would have you for my very own, but even more amazing, my first real friend is an Indian."

Will's feet automatically followed the little beaten dirt path that eventually led to the falls. His mind wandered, and he remembered back to when they first came to Thistle Canyon. He and his parents had been on their way to settle in the new land of California when their wagon broke down somewhere in the Utah Territory. It was March, and the winter weather was lingering longer than any of them liked. Ma was close to having a baby, and Pa decided they would be better off finding the settlements that were located somewhere down the long canyon. They could stay there until after the baby was born and still have time to put in a summer crop. When the weather turned warm next spring, they would then continue their journey to California.

Staring at the path ahead of him, Will remembered how after only two days into the canyon, disaster struck. One of their two horses stepped into a gopher hole and broke his leg.

"We're going to have to shoot him," Papa remarked *sadly.*

"No!" cried Will, *"Please try to help him. We need him!"*

Papa had no choice. He had to shoot the animal. That left the family with only one horse to pull the wagon down the steep canyon. The wagon was much too heavy for a single horse. Ma and Pa knew they would either have to abandon half of their belongings or find a closer place to settle. They decided to start out and see if the remaining horse could get them a little farther down the canyon.

By the middle of the day, Pa realized they couldn't make it to the settlements down in the far off valley. He felt it would be better to risk making a home somewhere close by than to chance throwing away items they may need to help them get through the next winter. Besides, summer would soon arrive, and they had to start making preparations to get some corn and wheat planted.

After scouting and exploring the area, Pa excitedly told the family he had found a meadow in a little valley to the east of where they were camped. There was a stream running through it, and it was protected by cliffs on two sides. The canyon walls would temper the strong winter winds. Best of all, the meadow had rich soil to plant their crops in.

Pa told them he had come across two men on horseback during his exploration. They told him there were small farms every five to ten miles stretching all the way down the canyon to the valley below. It was true the neighbors weren't very close, but at least they were there!

After struggling with the heavy wagon, the family finally made it to the little meadow and found the perfect place to make their home. The two settlers Pa had met brought their sons and helped them put up a small cabin. With their help the cabin went up fast, and by the end of April, Pa was clearing ground to plant seeds. Ma had her baby soon after and Will got a new little brother.

CHAPTER 4

The Meeting Place

Tat-a-tat-tat", the sharp, staccato beat of a woodpecker furiously pecking at a large pine tree brought Will back to the present.

The sun would be straight up in a couple of hours, but Will knew if he hurried he could pick a bucket of berries and leave them to cool in the middle of the stream. He would stop to pick them up again and bring them home after he met with Peteetneet.

By late morning, Will had filled the bucket with juicy, red currants. "Ma is gonna love these," he said to Tag as he stuffed another dripping handful into his mouth. The red juice left a stain that trailed from his lower lip to the bottom of his chin. It was almost lunch time, but Will decided he would save his lunch for later.

"I think we ate as many as we picked," he said to Tag. Will glanced at the sky. "The sun is almost straight up, boy. It's time to get going." Suddenly Will's stomach was doing flip-flops again. What if he doesn't come? he thought to himself. Worse yet, what if his people won't let him see me? I wonder if they like white people.

Will had heard all kinds of stories by the trail drivers about Indians who fought the white man. During his family's long trip west, they had not met one group of Indians. His Pa told him the Utes were usually very peaceful. They had strong ponies and made it their business to trade them with the warring Navajos, the Spanish across the Rio Grande, the Piutes, Hopi, and the white settlers in the area.

Will propped the big bucket between three large rocks in the middle of the cool stream. Next, he fashioned a lid with his straw hat to keep the birds out. After making sure the bucket was secure, he and Tag waded through the water to the other side.

In the distance, the pounding of great waves of water could be heard falling over the cliffs. Will's feet slipped on the wet grasses and mud as he followed the little stream toward the big river. He could feel the river long before he could see it. The steady throbbing of huge amounts of water falling over giant rocks seemed to give it a heartbeat. It was a living thing, exciting and full of life. The closer he got to the falls, the louder was the roar of her mighty waters. A feeling of awe swelled his chest when he looked at the sky and saw a rainbow floating in a watery mist just above the trees.

"Tag, Ma says a rainbow is a bridge to heaven. Do you believe it?" Will said thoughtfully as he turned to walk away.

At the junction of the little stream and the big river, Will stopped to find the narrow trail that led to the bottom of the falls. It was a deer trail and covered with brush and overhanging limbs. He didn't want to go the wrong way. As he started down the path, he picked up Tag and stuck him in the opening of his shirt. "Quit tickling me!" he said as he tried to stop the puppy from squirming. The path ran next to the falls, and he didn't want his rambunctious little dog falling off the edge. After picking his way down the face of the cliff, Will followed the path to a little pool that was on the inside of the waterfall. It was almost magical. On one side were the sheer walls of the cliff, and on the other he could look through a shimmering curtain of water that cascaded into the depths below. The huge rock that formed the back wall had big drops of water trickling down its granite face. The drops gathered together and made little rivulets winding through big patches of moss and ferns that were clinging persistently to its steep sides. When Will turned back around, he could look through the tumbling waters and spy at the river on the other side.

"Look, Tag, we're looking through a secret room. We can see out, but no one can see in!"

He knew he had to meet Peteetneet on the other side of the river so he meticulously began picking his way through the rocky pool. Carefully he chose each rock he stepped on but, the rocks were very slippery and Will caught himself falling more than once. He shivered. The icy cold water stung when it splashed on his skin.

Finally he reached the far edge of the little pool. He stayed close to the wall until he came out of the rocks on the other side of the river. Shading his eyes with his hand, he looked down the river past the falls to see if he could see Peteetneet. No one was there. He took Tag out of his shirt and set him on the ground.

"I don't see him, boy. Do you?" he asked the frisky puppy. Tag cocked his head to the side and, with a quizzical look in his eyes, gave a quick little bark. Will was disappointed, but then he remembered how the Indian had been hidden in the trees when Will first heard him call out. He wasn't able to see the other boy until he had deliberately stepped out and made himself visible. Will decided to make his way down this side of the river and find a place to stay put.

"I'm sure if we just wait a while, Peteetneet will find us," he said to the pup.

CHAPTER 5

Secrets Shared

Will wiggled his nose and breathed in deeply. It smelled like something was cooking, but he could not see a fire, or even any smoke. He got up from the log he was sitting on and looked carefully around at all the trees and boulders strewn along the side of the river. The smell was delicious, and he felt a tightness in his stomach.

"Maybe I am getting hungry now," he said as his eyes scanned the bushes that led into the forest. Suddenly, Will spied a bunch of quail feathers tied to a limb on a small aspen tree. He hurried over to the tree and touched the little bunch of feathers. There were three of them held together by a thin strip of rawhide and looped around a branch on the tree. Will took them off the limb and studied them carefully.

"These were put here on purpose," he said, "I think Peteetneet is trying to tell me something." Will looked up past the bushes and searched the trees and rocks in the distance. At least I hope it was him trying to tell me something! he thought to himself.

Sure enough on a big boulder straight ahead, he saw

another little grouping of feathers. He ran to the rock and saw the feathers were tied in the same way with another little strip of rawhide. This time the feathers lay on top of the boulder with a small rock holding them in place. They seemed to be pointing to a bend in the river.

"Come on, Tag, let's explore this," Will called to the puppy.

They started out in the direction the feathers were pointing. Will and Tag climbed over rocks and walked through thick bushes, until they reached a spot where the river took a sharp bend into a stand of tall cotton-wood trees. It was a shady and cool place. The trees had big thick trunks, and their leaves were chattering as they softly rubbed against each other in a gentle breeze. A big smile spread across Will's face when he spotted Peteetneet kneeling in front of a small, smokeless fire. On the fire, a fat rabbit was roasting on a spit.

"Little Bear found my message," Peteetneet said looking up at Will. "White boy have sharp eyes. That is good. We eat food now."

Will's face glowed at the compliment the *Ute-ah* had paid him. "Do you always cook your own food?" Will asked breathlessly, "This is great!"

"Mother and sisters prepare food, but everyone help gather and hunt. My job to catch rabbits. Grandfather call me Rabbit Racer, because not many rabbits get away from me. When hunting, many time I cook meal for myself. Now I cook for my friend, Little Bear."

Peteetneet opened a small pouch he had sitting on the ground next to him. He pulled out two wooden cups and handed one to Will. Will studied the cup and noticed it was made out of a knot of wood from a tree. Peteetneet then pulled a leg off of the rabbit and put it in Will's cup. He took another leg and started to eat it. Will lifted the meat to his lips.

"Ouch!" he whispered. It was hot and burned his tongue, but he smiled at the Indian as he chewed the juicy, tender food. When the meat hit his stomach, he realized just how hungry he really was and began to eat the rest of his meal with relish.

With a pleading look in his dark brown eyes, Tag jumped up and down in front of Will.

"You're hungry too aren't you, boy." Will said laughing and tossed him some scraps from the juicy rabbit meat.

It was a big rabbit, and the three of them ate until they were stuffed. Peteetneet passed Will a leather water bag to wash down the remains of the meal.

"Boy was that good," Will said. "Do you think you could teach me how you do that?" he asked Peteetneet.

"First you must catch rabbit," said the boy. "I teach you how to hunt, and later I show you how to cook."

Peteetneet took down the tripod he had cooked the meat on and carefully stashed the three pieces of wood into a small hole in the middle of a pile of rocks. He then scattered the ashes and put out the remaining coals. With a stick from a cottonwood tree, he carefully brushed the dirt until there was no trace of the fire.

Will watched with great interest. "Why are you getting rid of the ashes that way?" he asked Peteetneet.

"When Indian take something from Mother Earth,

he always say thanks. Me clean dirt and leave offering, then Mother Earth provide for us again." As he said these words, Peteetneet took a small acorn from his pouch and patted it carefully in the earth where their fire had been.

"I never thought of saying thanks to the earth before," Will pondered.

"Come, me show Little Bear how to catch *taboots* (rabbit). Must take meat back to village for Bear Dance ceremony."

Peteetneet picked up the small wooden cups, wiped them clean with some leaves, and stashed them with his tripod in the rocks.

"This is special meeting place for Indian and white boy—our secret. Me leave messages for Little Bear in rocks. Little Bear do same for Peteetneet."

"Agreed," said Will, "Let's shake on it!" Puzzled, Peteetneet looked at Will and asked, "What mean, 'shake on it'?"

Will held out his right hand. "Give me your hand," he said, and Peteetneet stretched his hand out to him. "Now shake," Will said as he vigorously started to pump Peteetneet's hand. "When two white men shake like this, it means you have made a promise and will keep it."

A smile lit up Peteetneet's face; he grabbed Will's hand and gave it a good hard shake.

"Where is your village from here, Peteetneet?" Will asked.

"Down river past place where white boy run from big mother bear. You come visit village today."

25

"Do you think your people will like me?"

"*Nuche* heap rich. Like Little Bear." said Peteetneet.

"*Nuche*? What does that mean? Does your tribe have a lot of money?"

"What is money?" asked Peteetneet. "*Nuche* word mean 'we the people,' in white boy language. When Indian is rich it mean he has many friends. Not good when one has no friends. That person is very poor. Come, we go now."

The two boys looked around, made sure nothing was left on the ground, and started towards a little trail in the trees.

"Come on, Tag," called Will. The trail wound parallel to the river through piles of rock and thick oak brush trees. Every now and then the boys would come to a fork in the path with the right side angling down toward the water. There were lots of deer droppings and small animal tracks in the dirt.

Soon the path came out of the brush into a big meadow. The grass was green, and brilliant wildflowers splashed the colors of a rainbow throughout the big field. Tag leaped up to a big sego lily and tried to bite the blossom off of the fragile flower.

Peteetneet stopped and looked carefully around. "This much good place to find rabbits," he said to Will. "*Ute-ah* have many way to hunt. Sometime we use bow and arrow, but I show Little Bear best way. First we make small fire."

Peteetneet started to gather small dried twigs, leaves, and pieces of bark. Will helped him clear a spot on the ground where they piled them into a small mound. The

Indian took two pieces of stone out of his pouch and began striking them together over the dried leaves.

"Those are nice pieces of flint," Will said as he watched Peteetneet. Soon sparks were flying onto the little pile. The edge of a leaf started to smolder and Peteetneet leaned over and blew gently onto the fragile tinder. Suddenly the leaf burst into flame, and Peteetneet started feeding other leaves into the flame. Will helped him add twigs and bark, until they had a nice little fire going all on its own.

"There are many way to hunt rabbit," said Peteetneet, "one easy way is when whole village get in big line and drive rabbits into pen made out of brush. With not so many people to help, we do it different way." Peteetneet had a bandoleer slung over his shoulder with a small bow, arrows, a sling shot and other hunting items in it. He reached in and took out the small skull of a rabbit's head, lifted the skull to his mouth, and started to blow through it. Will jumped at the sound. A haunting cry began to float through the air.

Startled, Will asked, "What was that?" Peteetneet smiled at the surprised look on Will's face.

"When rabbit hear sound, he think it from other injured rabbit and is curious. He come out of his hole to find out. If no rabbit come, then we take bunch of sticks, bind them together and make smoking torch. We hold smoke in front of rabbit hole, and rabbits come out for air."

"My pa just makes little traps with food in them for the rabbits. I never thought of using smoke," said Will.

"Rabbit make warm clothing for little children. Also, much good food." Peteetneet had his hair in braids. He lifted one of the braids and pointed to the rabbit tail hanging on the end of it. A rawhide strip secured the tail firmly in place.

"Good hunter earn right to wear tail in his hair. More hunts, more honor," said Peteetneet.

The boys stood up and started to gather a small bundle of dried twigs. Peteetneet took a green vine and wrapped it around the bunch of twigs and secured them together. He handed Will the bundle.

"White boy light sticks with fire," he said. Will bent over and held the sticks in the small flame, until they were steadily burning. The few leaves in the twigs were green and made a lot of smoke.

Peteetneet put his finger to his mouth and motioned Will to be quiet. He picked up the rabbit skull and walked silently into the meadow. Lifting the skull to his mouth, he blew through it, and the shrill, squealing sound penetrated the stillness of the area. Sure enough, about fifty feet in front of the Indian, a rabbit darted through the grass and then disappeared down a hole in the ground.

Peteetneet motioned Will to follow as he silently walked toward the place the rabbit disappeared. He squatted down and carefully ran his hand through the grasses. Suddenly his hand stopped, and he moved some of the weeds to reveal a small, dark hole going into the ground. He pointed to the hole and motioned Will to bring the firebrand closer. Will brought the sticks close to the opening and shoved the top down inside. Soon smoke was coming out all over the place. The boys left the bundle of sticks and inched their way away from the hole.

Peteetneet's eyes quickly scanned the area around them. He reached into his bandoleer and pulled out a small sling. It was a long, thin strip of leather with a rock balanced right in the middle. Suddenly, about fifteen feet away, the rabbit popped out of another hole.

"Look!" Will hissed as he pointed his finger. Quick as lightning, Peteetneet stood up and swung his sling around his head. He took careful aim and then let the sling fly swiftly through the air. Will's eyes almost popped out when he saw the middle of the sling hit the rabbit right on the head. The rabbit fell to the ground so quickly that Will was sure the animal never knew what had hit him.

The boys ran over to the rabbit. Peteetneet knelt down and felt for a heartbeat.

"Must make sure rabbit is dead and not stunned," he said to Will. Peteetneet then went over to the rabbit hole and stomped out the fire on the smoking sticks. He reached into the little leather pouch he carried at his waist, knelt down by the hole and put a small, round piece of buckskin next to the opening.

"Rabbit, excuse me for taking your life, but my family is hungry," he said.

Will looked a little puzzled, and Peteetneet explained.

"Long ago, Grandfather tell me all living things have spirit and are creatures of whole universe. Earth does not belong to man, but man belongs to earth.

Rabbit gave us food and skin for warmth, we thank Creator for gifts. When time for Indian to meet Creator, we must come to him without shame."

Will shook his head in amazement. He had never before thought about the earth giving him gifts. He just took it for granted that things would always be there when he needed them, and if they were there he could have them when he wanted. It made Will feel a little bit ashamed. He thought about all the beautiful currants he picked for his Ma that morning. It was natural to him that they should just be there for the taking. He was determined that from this time on he would be aware of the gifts of the earth and somehow try to show his thanks.

"Come, Little Bear, I take you to my village now," Peteetneet said as he gathered up his belongings and stuck them back into the bandoleer.

"I'll carry the rabbit for you," Will offered as he picked it up by the hind legs and followed the Indian through the meadow.

"Where are you, Tag" he called. The puppy came running to Will from the other side of the meadow and sniffed curiously at the rabbit dangling from Will's hand

CHAPTER 6

Yuta Village

Peteetneet led the way on a narrow deer trail. It wound snake-like through trees and rocks but never lost sight of the river. Will followed the Indian and was amazed at how quickly and quietly the boy could move. His moccasins stepped silently on the ground through twigs and dead leaves. Will glanced up at a tree when a robin started to sing. He looked back, and Peteetneet was nowhere to be seen.

"Wait!" Will called out in surprise. How could I lose sight of him so fast? he thought.

"Yikes!" Will yelped as Peteetneet jumped out from behind the tree right next to him.

"Little Bear must watch always," Peteetneet said,

"Never know when enemy be close."

"How did you do that?" Will asked. "I never even saw you disappear. Suddenly you were just gone!"

Peteetneet laughed at Will's amazement. "Indian very good at blending into Mother Earth. We become as one. Many time enemy walk right by. Now, Little Bear, close eyes and turn around very slow. Then open eyes, look in trees and find Peteetneet."

Peteetneet pointed to a small grassy spot that contained several big rocks and a scattering of aspen trees. "Must look with eyes like eagle," he said.

Will stayed where he was and turned slowly around. I'll find him this time, he thought. He can't hide from me when I know where he's going to be.

He stopped turning when he was facing the same direction he had started from. Squinting his eyes, he looked carefully into the area where Peteetneet told him to search. The grass was still, and there were no footprints bending the delicate stalks. With a frown, Will put his hand over his eyes to shade them from the glare of the sun. He looked at the gray and brown rocks scattered about on the ground and then searched among the white trunks of the aspen trees. Everything was still. He must be tricking me, Will thought.

"Okay, Peteetneet," Will called. "You said you would be in front of me, but I know you're not there."

Suddenly, one of the brown and gray rocks lying just ten feet from him moved and stood up. Will watched Peteetneet change from a small boulder to the Indian boy now walking towards him. A big grin cracked the brown cheeks of the Indian as he saw the look of surprise that was frozen on Will's face.

"How in tarnation did you do that?" Will said.

"Must be very still. Become like rock," said Peteetneet. "Indian fathers, grandfathers and great-grandfathers had to be much good at blending into land, so they could hunt animals. Food for village depends on it. If Indian in danger and cannot run, Indian crawl into brush or fold up on ground and be mistaken for rock. Indian's dark hair and clothing made from deer blend into earth colors and hide Indian. White boy with hair the color of sun much harder to hide. If Little Bear practice he will find way to become one with earth. Peteetneet help him."

"Come, follow," Peteetneet said as he left the trail and disappeared over the ridge of a little hill.

Not to be left behind, Will raced up the small hill after his friend. After topping the ridge, Will heard the whistle of a whippoorwill. He looked to his right and saw Peteetneet down on his hands and knees in a crouch. Peteetneet opened his mouth, and the perfect, clear tones of the whippoorwill call came floating from his lips. Delighted at the signal, Will quickly fell to his hands and knees and scooted over to the Indian's side.

"Whenever man go over ridge, he drop down to hands and knees close to ground. Must then go quickly, like small fox, along inside of ridge. Indian then get far away before enemy or animal know what happen to him," said Peteetneet. Quietly he turned around. Keeping his body rounded and low to the ground, he leaned into the side of the low ridge and quickly followed its rim to the top of a small hill. Will followed

Peteetneet, but he felt very awkward dragging the rabbit and stumbling over roots and small twigs that were in his way. It was a struggle to keep up.

When he caught up with Peteetneet, the Indian smiled and said, "Little Bear do good job. Soon be quick like Rabbit Racer."

Will wiped away the sweat that was trickling down into his eyes and smiled gratefully back at his friend.

Peteetneet stood up and looked out over the edge of the hill. Will followed him and beheld a sight that only a few months ago he never would have believed he would ever see. The river was so wide at the base of the hill that the rushing current from above was slowed to a gentle crawl. Like a big pot of honey that had tipped over on its side, the golden, sun drenched waters spread lazily out to faraway banks. Neatly lined up along the shoreline were about a dozen bark canoes. In the lake-like water, children were laughing, and women stood washing clothes. A small path led from its banks to the village about a hundred yards away. Will was speechless as he looked at the tepees sprawled out before him.

"This *Yuta* village," said Peteetneet with a wide sweep of his arm.

Will's heart quickened as he followed Peteetneet down the grassy hill. Some of the boys in the river spotted them and stopped their play. They began pointing and hollering words that Will didn't understand. Soon the girls and women were also staring at them.

"My people are much surprised to see white boy come into village. Do not fear. *Yuta* are peaceful people. Not hurt friend who come in peace," said

Peteetneet when he saw the anxious look on Will's face.

Will took a deep breath and let the air out slowly. He refused to let Peteetneet know how nervous he felt. "I'm fine," he said, "I've just never seen an Indian village before. At school my friends and I would talk about how the Indian people live, but it isn't anything like I imagined."

As Will followed Peteetneet he noticed the village had been placed close enough to the river, so the people had plenty of fresh water. The ground the tepees were on was a little higher than the river. Beyond the tepees, a forest of pine and aspen trees stretched out as far as Will could see. The trees would protect the village from bad winds whenever a storm came. Will could see that much thought had gone into picking their summer camp. He remembered again how his father had told him that the Ute Indians were nomadic and moved their villages to different locations in the summer and winter times.

"Come, I take Little Bear to meet Grandfather. He much good medicine man," said Peteetneet.

As the boys walked into the village, a group of small children followed them. Will smiled at them as they giggled and laughed amongst themselves. Peteetneet squared his shoulders and walked proudly in front of Will. The tepees were grouped orderly with all the doors facing east.

"Why don't you face your doors towards each other, so you can visit better?" Will asked.

"Door face east, so Indian can welcome new day," said Peteetneet.

Halfway through the village maze, Peteetneet stopped at a large tepee. He took the rabbit from Will and set it to the side of the doorway.

"This *kan-ne-ga* of Peteetneet mother. Little Bear meet." Will raised his eyebrows and looked at his friend with a very puzzled look on his face. "*Kan-ne-ga* mean sitting or staying place in Indian talk," said Peteetneet.

"You mean this is your home?" asked Will.

"Yes, 'home'—white man word. This Peteetneet's home," said the Indian. "*Kan-ne-ga* belong to squaw. Squaw make it, squaw put it up, squaw take it down when Indian move camp. Man is honored guest in squaw's home."

Peteetneet parted the deer hide covering on the door and stepped inside. He motioned for Will to follow him. Will had to wait a second for his eyes to adjust to the dim light. He noticed the only light available was coming from the doorway they had just entered and a small hole at the top of the tepee. He looked carefully and saw a wrinkled old man with two snow white long braids sitting in front of a fire opposite the door. As his eyes continued to adjust he saw a woman, whom Will correctly guessed was Peteetneet's mother. She stood up from where she was sitting on the left side of the old man.

"*Mike pe-en*," Peteetneet said to the woman.

"*Mike* Peteetneet," the woman replied back.

"*Mike too/woo chin*," Peteetneet said to the old man on the other side of the fire.

The man stood up slowly and turned to Will, "*Ahnah ne/gut?*" and then, "*Noo ne ki?*"

Puzzled, Will glanced at Peteetneet and then answered the old man.

"Uh, I'm sorry, but I don't speak Indian," he said. A slow smile crossed the man's face as he asked Peteetneet another question. Will found himself clenching and unclenching his fists. In spite of the reassurances Peteetneet had given him, he didn't know if this man was welcoming him or not. Peteetneet answered the old man in the Ute tongue and then turned to Will.

"Medicine man have place of honor," said Peteetneet. "Yellow Jacket is village medicine man. Grandfather much old and much wise. Little Bear meet Grandfather."

Without realizing it, Will found he had been holding his breath. He quietly let the air go out of his lungs and put his hand out to the old man. "Hello, sir," he said.

The man lifted his frail, wrinkled hand to the white boy and shook hands with him. Speaking English, the grandfather then said, "Indian greet boy as white man do. Grandson bring boy to village as friend. Grandfather welcome friend of Peteetneet. You be friend of village from this day forth. We shake on it," he said as he pumped Will's hand a second time.

Will grinned and felt much better. Peteetneet must have told his grandfather about Will and prepared him for this meeting. In spite of his earlier fears, he found himself feeling a genuine friendship with this old man.

"This is my mother," Peteetneet said taking Will's arm and turning him toward the woman who stood on the other side of his grandfather. "She does not speak the white man tongue but want you to know you are welcome in her *kan-ne-ga*."

In a welcoming gesture, Peteetneet's mother dipped her head ever so slightly and lowered her eyes at the same time. She then gave Will a big smile. Will smiled back and said, "*Mike*," the Ute word for "hello". The woman raised her eyebrows and with another smile said, "*Mike*, Little Bear."

While they were walking to the village, Will had asked Peteetneet to teach him a Ute greeting, so he would be able to say something in the Indian language when he met Peteetneet's people. He was grateful he had at least learned this one simple word.

As Will looked at the people around him, he was amazed at the gentle kindnesses he had received in their presence. He felt embarrassed as he thought back to the time when he lived in Boston and was going to school. He and his friends had thought Indians were all savages and were not as good as white people. They figured because the Indians lived in tepees they weren't smart enough to build houses. Because of that and other differences none of them really understood, they just figured the white men were better and had every right to move the Indians off of the lands they owned. Besides, how could they own the land? They hadn't bought it from anyone, and the government hadn't given it to them, they had reasoned. He now wished he could show his old friends how wrong all of them had been.

CHAPTER 7

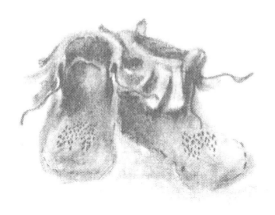

Squash Head's Anger

Carefully holding the soft, beautiful moccasins in his hands, Will ducked his head and stepped out of the tepee. The slippers were made of deer hides that had been worked and tanned until they had attained the softness and golden color of the finest leather. They were hand-stitched and had an intricate design on the top made out of tiny beads depicting a small bear cub. Will stood up and examined them in awe. This gift from Peteetneet's sister had truly astonished him.

He had only met Tabiona an hour ago when Peteetneet introduced him to his family. Her long, shiny black hair was pulled back with a leather band around her forehead. She was dressed in a simple deer-hide dress that hung just below her knees. In her hands she held a pair of leather moccasins she was sewing a pattern of beads on.

"*My brother tell me you play with little bear,*" *Tabiona said, smiling.*

"*Oh no!*" *groaned Will.* "*Did he tell everybody?*"

Tabiona laughed, "*Mother bear must think white boy a friend. It be easy for her to make dinner out of him.*" *She smiled again and said,* "*Me think this good sign. Look at moccasin I work on,*" *she said as she held up her sewing.*

"*How did you do this?*" *he said.* "*Where did you get these beads?*"

Peteetneet grinned at his friend's wonder. Then he said, "*White man trade many beads and other things for Indian ponies. My sister has gift from Creator to make beads turn into special pictures.*"

"*Wow, would I love to have a pair of these,*" *said Will.*

Tabiona picked up the other moccasin and shyly held the pair of them out to Will.

"*Tabiona much honored if white boy accept moccasins from her,*" *she said. Blushing a deep red, he declined. But Peteetneet touched his arm and when Will looked into the boy's eyes, he noticed a determined look and a slight nod of the head that seemed to tell him to take the gift.*

Will felt the sun getting hot on his back. He glanced back at the tepee. Peteetneet needed to stay a little longer and talk with his grandfather, so Will started walking back toward the river. There he would wait for him in the shade of a cottonwood tree.

"Come on, Tag!" Will called out to his dog. Tag was sniffing at a rack of fish drying in the sun. He looked at Will with a question in his eyes and then, wagging his tail, bounded after his master.

The white boy walked through the small village self-consciously trying to ignore the stares from the women and small children. When he reached the trees near the river, he stepped down the sloping incline toward the water. On the mossy bank Will found a nice spot to sit in the grass. As he stared out at the water and watched some children splashing and playing in the distance, Will felt a great sense of tranquility. His life now was so different from the life he and his family had left behind just a short time ago.

"White boy much brave to visit village where not wanted."

Startled, Will jumped to his feet and spun around. Standing in front of him was an Indian boy with his arms folded and a menacing frown on his face. He was built quite stockily and had a very large head, round as a squash. In his mouth, a big set of teeth gleamed bright enough to make a beaver proud. He was at least two years older than Will. Behind him stood two other boys, equally as intimidating and in seeming support of their friend.

Surprised at the boy's negative remarks, Will stammered, "Wait—you—you don't understand! I came with Peteetneet. He invited me! He is my friend!"

"Ummgh. White man not Indian friend," said the boy in a stern and unfriendly voice. White man take Indian hunting ground and chase away animals. White man stop in Indian summer camp and put wooden tepee up with big fence all around. He plant his corn and never leave. Indian have to find new summer camp for his people. Not good. White man have no right to take Indian land. Now white boy come to camp and take Indian moccasin from Tabiona. Me, Squash Head, not like!"

Will stared in disbelief at the three boys. Peteetneet had assured him his people were friendly and would welcome Will into their camp. He wasn't prepared for this kind of a confrontation.

Suprised, Will looked down at the moccasins he was holding in his hand. "What do you mean by 'take'?" he said to the angry boy in front of him. "Tabiona gave me these as a gift! I tried to turn her down, but she insisted!"

"Girl must insist," said Squash Head, "not polite to keep possession when other person want. White boy much rude."

"Do you mean because I said I liked them and would like to have a pair she felt she had to give them to me?" asked Will with uncertainty.

"Boy rude to ask. Tabiona could not refuse."

Will was speechless as he stared at the three boys in front of him. He didn't know what to do. He had no idea that just saying he liked something would cause a person to feel as though they had to give it to him.

"I'm sorry," Will said. "I did not understand your ways."

"Sorry not good enough," blurted Squash Head, "white boy leave and not come back!"

"That's not fair," Will said indignantly, "I will apologize to Tabiona and explain that I did not understand."

Sensing the anger in the Indian boy, Tag ran in front

of Will and started barking at Squash Head.

"Stupid dog," Squash Head shouted as he kicked Tag in the ribs and sent him sailing head over heels into the bushes. "Not good for anything but dinner pot!"

"Tag! Are you all right?" cried Will as he ran to untangle his dog from the branches. Tag was yipping and had an ugly gash in his side.

"It's all right, boy," said Will as he gently laid him in some soft grass. Angrily he turned around to face his tormentor.

"Look at white boy and his baby," said Squash Head to his two friends while pointing and laughing at Will. "He make much good squaw!" The two boys started hooting and dancing around in circles. "Dog Squaw! Dog Squaw!" they hooted and hollered while Squash Head continued laughing.

Clenching his fists into hard little balls, Will said, "Stop it. Stop it right now!" The boys only continued laughing and hooting all the louder.

Suddenly Will ducked into a crouch, ran with all his might, and tackled Squash Head right below the knees. With surprise etched on his face, Squash Head teetered and started to fall backwards from the sudden blow. He threw his arms up into the air and reached frantically for anything to stop him from toppling over the edge of the bank and into the river. Empty air was all there was to grasp, and losing his balance he fell with a huge thud into the water and mud below.

Startled at his own daring, Will jumped up and stared at Squash Head who was lying there too surprised to move. The other two boys had stopped dancing around and looked at Will with astonishment. It was evident that no one had ever dared challenge Squash Head before.

"You be sorry now!" said Panawick, one of Squash Head's two friends. The other friend, Black Horse, nodded vigorously in agreement.

Suddenly Squash Head came leaping up with mud, leaves and water flying in every direction.

"Yaaargh!" he yelled as he came charging at Will, holding a big stick in his hand. Will took two steps back and looked around for something to defend himself with. His stomach lurched, and fear drove bile up into his throat. His eyes widened as he saw Squash Head muttering angrily while he stumbled and fell trying to get up the muddy bank. Get a hold of yourself, Will thought while planting his feet on the ground to steady himself for the blow that was surely coming.

"Stop!" A powerful voice filled with authority called out. All the boys froze and turned to see where the sound came from. Standing at the top of the incline stood Peteetneet and his grandfather, Yellow Jacket, the respected tribal medicine man.

"Squash Head, Panawick and Black Horse must learn manners. White boy guest of Peteetneet and welcome in village. You pick berries with women for rest of day. When boy acts like warrior he is man and hunts with other braves. When boy acts like child he help women in field. When sun sleeps, Yellow Jacket ask Great Spirit if boys learn lesson. When sun wakes to new day, boys come to medicine man tent."

All three boys hung their heads in humiliation and

started walking towards the village. Will held his breath as they started to leave. As Squash Head passed by Will, he glanced at him and a small glint of anger flashed in his eyes. Will knew in his heart that no matter how many berries Squash Head picked he would still have to finish what was started today.

Peteetneet hurried over to Will, "Is Little Bear all right?" he asked with concern in his eyes. "Yes," Will sighed, "I'm sorry about all this, but Squash Head kicked Tag and I couldn't help myself!"

Will walked over to his pet and picked him up. Tag whimpered in his arms and snuggled up safely to Will's chest.

"Come," said Yellow Jacket, "I help you fix dog and make him better." Silently, both boys followed Yellow Jacket back to the village and the medicine man's tepee.

CHAPTER 8

An Ancient Friendship

Will sat down in the coolness of the tepee and blinked his eyes, trying to adjust to the semi-darkness. Yellow Jacket picked up a piece of square cloth, dumped some sand into the middle of it, and then tied the corners together into a tight knot. Will watched with curiosity as the medicine man then put the ball of sand into a pot of melted fat where the fat soon saturated the sand. Next, he lashed the ball to a sturdy stick and stuck it in the ground. Taking a small brand from the coals of last night's fire, Yellow Jacket held the glowing ember to the ball of sand and fat. It quickly took fire and the tepee soon filled with a soft, glowing light.

"Well, I'll be!" Will exclaimed. "I'll have to tell my Pa how to do that."

Yellow Jacket smiled at Will's words. "We must help

little dog now," he said. "Little Bear hold dog so I fix good."

Will held Tag tightly in his arms and turned him on his side, so the medicine man could work on the ugly abrasion on Tag's upper leg. Yellow Jacket took two of his fingers and scooped something out of a small clay pot. Will watched as he carefully smeared the yellow paste all over the wound.

"What is that stuff?" Will asked. "Will it make it better?"

"This rabbit fat mixed with healing plant," said Yellow Jacket. "It keep wound soft and has power to make better very fast."

Will smiled gratefully at the old man. "Thank you," he said, "Tag is part of our family and I'm responsible for him. I don't like to see him hurt."

Peteetneet had watched silently while Grandfather was doing his work. He now spoke in the Ute tongue, "Grandfather, it would make my heart very happy for Little Bear to come to Bear Ceremony. I ask your permission."

Grandfather looked thoughtfully at the two boys and sat down next to them. "My grandson ask for you to see Bear Dance," he said in English, looking at Will. "Sit, and I will give you a telling."

Will and Peteetneet slid over by Grandfather and waited expectantly for him to begin.

"Many, many suns ago, long before Yellow Jacket came to live with this people and even long before Yellow Jacket's grandfather came to live with this people, a Ute brave had a dream. It was in the springtime when the melting ice and snow were freeing mother earth from their tight hold," Grandfather said. "The brave dreamed that in his travels he came upon a big sleeping bear who had not awakened from his winter dreams. Ute brave knew it very late in spring for bear to still be sleeping. If he did not awaken soon he maybe starve. So Indian wake him from his long winter nap. As a reward for Ute's kindness, the bear took him to special place deep in woods where all other bears were dancing to celebrate end of winter. Bear invited brave to dance with them, and he taught the man his sacred dance. Ute brave then return to his people, and he taught them bear dance. Now our people always greet new springtime and awakening of bears with sacred dance to celebrate our ancient friendship."

Peteetneet looked at Will and said, "Ever since that time, our people have helped the bear to wake in the springtime. Our dance will last for the passing of four suns. At that time, the bears are awake, have found mates and have much food to eat."

"Do you dance for four whole days without stopping?" Will asked.

Yellow Jacket looked at Will and said with a serious look. "Bears grateful for friendship of our people. When we finish with *Mamaqui Mowats* , the bear ceremony, they repay *Ute-ah* by assisting us in practice of our magic. Bear is wisest and bravest of all animals except for his fearful friend, mountain lion. He possesses wonderful magic powers. When Mother Earth send us white bear, it is strong magic and has special meaning. You are white man's son, and bear has accepted you as one of his own. This very rare. If not so, you would have been killed by mother bear when my grandson first see you. The Great Spirit tells me you are sent to us for special purpose. Your name, Little Bear is very powerful. One day we will find out what you are chosen for."

Will's eyes got bigger as he listened to these last words.

Peteetneet turned to Will, "Our ceremony last four days. If Little Bear come on last day he will see the bear come out of his cave and join my people in feasting and games." Turning to Yellow Jacket, he asked, "Will that please you, Grandfather?"

CHAPTER 9

Picture Talk

"For the earth he drew a straight line,
For the sky a bow above it;
White the space between for day-time,
Filled with little stars for night time;
On the left a point for sunrise,
On the right a point for sunset,
On the top a point for noontide,
And for rain and cloudy weather
Waving lines descending from it."

(*From* <u>Hiawatha</u> *by* *Longfellow*)

William kicked small rocks and clumps of dirt as he followed the path behind Peteetneet. His mind was reeling with all the things that had happened to him this past day. He had learned so many new things and, unfortunately, even made an enemy all in one short afternoon. Yesterday my life was much simpler, he thought. Peteetneet's voice snapped Will out of his musings.

"Little Bear, we almost to waterfall. We must go to place where I leave you message to come to Bear

Dance," he said.

"How do I leave you a message?" Will asked. "I can write pretty good, but do you know the white man's way of writing? Should I make some code out of feathers or something?"

Peteetneet laughed. "Indian not make funny scratches on paper like white man!" he said. "We not need. When something important must be remembered, our fathers tell their children the telling. The children will then tell their children the telling, and this telling will always be in tribe. Sometime Indian must leave message for others not with him. Grandfathers from long ago make picture stories, so they can do this. This how Peteetneet leave Will message. I make my picture telling on bark of tree or soft piece of buffalo skin. Peteetneet teach Little Bear how to make. "

"You learn everything from stories?" Will asked. "We go to school to learn."

"Stories much good," Peteetneet said, "All good things learned in stories. Much easy to remember. Indian like stories very much," he said while pointing to himself.

The boys reached the little clearing by the river at the base of the waterfall where Will had met Peteetneet for lunch. "Sit down, Little Bear. You remember where Peteetneet keep cooking tool in hole of rock? This is place where we leave messages. I teach you picture story, and Little Bear know what message means."

Will sat on the ground, and Peteetneet picked up a sharp stick. "I show you how story go," he said as he drew a large circle in the dirt in front of him.

"Story begin with picture in middle of circle. Then you must read picture on the left side of middle picture. Then picture to left of that picture, until you have followed pictures all way around circle and you get to last picture. "Like this," he said while pointing to the picture circle he had drawn in the dirt.

"I think I understand. You read the pictures going backwards from the inside out," Will said.

"Yes," said Peteetneet. "But, when I send Little Bear picture story I put moon in corner of message so he know when to come."

Will wrinkled his brow, not sure what Peteetneet meant by that.

"Ummm, what do you call the time from one full moon to another?" he asked Will.

"A month," said Will.

"Yes, a month. What does white man call this month?"

"You mean the month we are in now?" asked Will.
"Yes."

"We call this month May."

"To our people it is Planting Moon," said Peteetneet. "See five lines next to moon? This show it is fifth sun of planting Moon. Peteetneet always put suns on picture message so Little Bear know which sun Indian want to meet him."

"I get it!" Will said. "What do you call June? I mean, the month after the Planting Moon?"

"Rose Moon is next month after Planting Moon," said Peteetneet.

"Okay, so I put a rose over the top of the moon. Is it like this?" Will asked.

"Yes!" Peteetneet said delighted.

"Little Bear understand!"

"I put nine lines by the moon so it means it is the ninth day of the Rose Moon! Am I right?" Will asked.

"Yes, nine lines mean ninth sun, or day, of Rose Moon. Little Bear very smart," said Peteetneet.

"But," said Will, "I don't understand all those pictures you put in your circle. What do they mean?"

"Each picture tell story. This story about two brothers named Spotted Elk and White Beaver who go through very bad winter and three member of tribe freeze to death. They are very hungry and little girl gets sick, but medicine man cannot fix. She die. Everyone very sad. The chief say very soon sun come out and weather get warm. The buffalo come, and they have plenty food. What he said true, and in three day the look out see buffalo. They get very much meat and dry it on drying poles. They a happy people. But they not forget little girl, and they place flag of sorrow on little girl grave," said Peteetneet.

"Wow!" said Will. "Do you think I could ever learn how to do these pictures?"

Peteetneet laughed. "Not so fast, Little Bear. Must learn picture slowly. Right now I teach you only picture you need to send message to Peteetneet," he said pointing to himself. "I give you more picture later."

Peteetneet reached into his pouch and pulled out a small piece of tanned leather. With some black charcoal, he drew a group of pictures he wanted Will to learn.

Will was amazed at the speed with which the Indian boy drew his pictures. But as he watched his friend, Will began to realize that it wasn't any different from when he was writing in English. He never thought about how fast he could write his letters, so why should Peteetneet not be able to make his picture writing go just as quickly?

Peteetneet grinned at Will. "I make these picture on buffalo hide for you," he said. "Take home and study picture. When Little Bear need to see his friend, he make picture for Peteetneet and leave it in rock. I find and understand. In time it be very easy for you to do."

Will looked at the pictures on the piece of leather. They were some of the same ones Peteetneet had drawn in the dirt.

"Agreed," said Will not quite as sure of himself as

his friend seemed to be of him.

"When time for Bear Dance, Peteetneet leave message here in rock. You come!" he said. "Now I walk white boy to his mother's *Ken-ne-ga*."

"Great, I want you to meet my parents," said Will, "but first I must pick up the currants I left in the stream for my mother."

"Boy pick currants for his mother?" said Peteetneet. "That squaw work!"

Will smiled. "White people don't think of it as girl's work," he said. "It's just one of my chores. Besides, my pa says it's an honor for a man to make a woman's work easier. They're not as strong as we are."

Peteetneet looked at Will to see if he was joking with him. The Indian realized with surprise that Will was very serious.

"Hey, you ought to try it sometime. It would probably shock your ma, but it sure would be fun to see the look on her face. Besides, it will make you feel good inside."

Will laughed at the puzzled look on Peteetneet's face. The Indian boy had wrinkled his brow and was staring at him.

In exasperation, Will kicked at a rock. "Ah, come on, Pete," he said using the nickname he had given his friend, "Let's get going."

When Will got home he took a pencil and carefully wrote down all the names of the pictures Peteetneet had drawn for him. He was determined to learn the picture language of the *Ute-ah* people.

Peteetneet

Bear Alive

Bear Dead

Bear Ceremony

Medicine Plants

Bear Glad Heart

Bear Sad Heart

Wounded Bear

Little Bear

Two Eagles

Chief Standing Bear

I or Me

Two Brothers

Medicine Man

Little Girl

Bow and Arrow

Left Teepee

Big Voice

Peace Pipe

Come

Power

Grave Flag

Falling Leaf Moon

Rose Moon

Night Time

Sunrise

Noon

Sunset

Sun

Great Spirit Everywhere

56

Three Years	Fish	River	Indian Camp	Canoe
Buffalo	Woman	Send Signal	Encampment	Bad Spirit Medicine
TeePee	Forest	Fear	Man With Gun	Dead Man
Grieves	Bad	Talk Together	Run	Discovery
Hear	See	Rest	Same Tribe	Rabbit
Traveled	Horse	Speak Lies	Wise Man	Plenty Corn

CHAPTER 10

Will's Gift

"OUCH! That burned my fingers!" Will flinched as he jerked his hand back. "It's your own fault," his mother replied calmly, "I told you to wait until the candy had cooled for a few minutes before you started to pull it."

Will looked away with a sheepish look on his face and plopped down on a wooden stool next to the big pine table that filled most of the kitchen area. "I can't wait to go check and see if Peteetneet has left me a message. He said the bear dance lasted four days, and tomorrow will be the fourth day. He said I could come for the fourth day! Why haven't I heard from him yet?" Will said in exasperation.

"Be patient, boy. We're almost finished here, and you can go check for your message. I'll just bet it's there today," said his mother. "Now help me finish this candy."

Will stood up and added a dab more of butter to his

hands. He picked up the ball of honey candy and started to pull and stretch it. Soon it reached a soft golden color. Will twisted it into a long rope and laid it out on the table top. He picked up a butcher knife and started chopping the hardened strand of candy into bite-size pieces.

"Ma, can I give Tabiona one of the currant pies you just finished making? I want to give her something special, since she gave me those bear moccasins," Will said.

"No, Will, I want you to give this pie to her mother. We need to send something that will contribute to their feast," she said.

"But Ma!"

"I'll tell you what, you can take some of this candy and give it to your friend. It will be something she has never tasted before, and I promise you she will like it very much," Mother said.

"Great idea!" Will said.

Will's mother got into her sewing basket and brought out a scrap of bright calico material. She tore the material into a square and put a handful of the hard candy into the middle of the cloth. She then brought up the four corners and tied them into a snug square knot. It looked bright and cheerful.

"Thank you!" Will said and ran for the cabin door, "I've got to go check now and see if there is a message. I'll be back soon," he said while tossing his ma a quick wave good-bye.

Will would not be disappointed. The message was waiting for him at the appointed place.

CHAPTER 11

The Message Comes

Will waited impatiently at the bottom of the waterfall. After finding the message the day before, he had wasted no time in preparing to meet Peteetneet the next morning. He held the small piece of leather tightly in his hand. Looking down at the scrap of skin, he once again read the picture-words Peteetneet had written.

(Little Bear - Come - Sunrise - Indian Camp - Bear Ceremony - Planting Moon on the 9th day)

Will was proud of himself for being able to understand the message. When Peteetneet had first told him about the picture language, Will was afraid he would not be able to learn it. Most of all, he didn't want Peteetneet to think he wasn't smart enough to figure it out. But he had carefully studied the crude drawings his friend had made for him and practiced making the pictures. Soon he found he had memorized the drawings and could make a pretty good rendition of the pictures himself.

The message told him to be at their meeting place by sun-up. Will had been so excited to come that he'd left while it was still pitch dark.

Snapping out of his thoughts, Will looked at the hills to the east of him. Bright yellow rays of light were reaching over the tops of the trees. The sun was close behind and soon the dim light of night would turn into bright daylight. "He should be here soon," Will said aloud.

"Little Bear," a voice said behind him. Startled, Will whirled around and found a grinning Peteetneet standing there.

"You're here!" Will said.

"White boy early," Peteetneet said, "beat Indian."

"I didn't want to miss a single thing," Will's words rushed out. "I couldn't sleep very well, so I decided to leave even though I knew I might get here before you."

The Indian smiled at Will's excitement. It pleased him very much that Will wanted to be a part of his people's sacred ceremony.

"Grandfather almost never let outsider view Bear Dance. Peteetneet very happy Will understand how important it is to the *Ute-ah*," he said. "Come now, we go." He turned and started walking on the path that led to the village.

Will slung the parcel of gifts he was carrying over

his shoulder. He adjusted the knapsack carefully so the pie would not be damaged and quickly followed after the Indian.

"Pete, will you tell me what has happened these last few days?" Will asked his friend. As they walked, Peteetneet started to fill Will in.

"Grandfather told you we must help bear wake from long winter sleep. Our people prepare many suns for start of dance. First, we build *a-vik-wok-et,* or as you would say, a cave of sticks. Cave very big and round like bear cave. It has only one opening that face the sun where she rise in morning. Walls of cave made of pine branches and almost twice as tall as Grandfather. Top is open to Father Sky."

"Gosh," said Will, "it must be very big if all your people can fit in it!"

"Yes, whole village fit in cave," said Peteetneet, "singers and drum beaters sit in one end of cave. This much honor for them, because their chanting awaken bears. They chosen at birth as were their fathers and their fathers before them. Each father teach son ceremonial chants and how to play instruments. Sometimes everyone know songs. But only braves allowed to sing."

"My mother wouldn't like that," said Will, "She likes to sing too much."

Peteetneet smiled and said, "Music echo very loudly in ceremonial cave. It become sound of thunder and wake sleeping bears in their mountain caves. Ceremony lasts four suns and one moon. This is time needed by bears to recover from long winter sleep.

"Today is fourth sun and bears will all be awake and

will eat and find their mates. We celebrate with them with great feast and many contest. Bear very grateful to their brothers, the *Ute-ah.*"

"Will I get to hear the singing and see the dancing?" Will asked.

"Oh yes, Little Bear. The feast does not start until sun is past highest part of sky."

When they reached the top of the ridge and looked down into the little valley nestled in the bend of the river, the boys paused and watched the excitement below them. The ceremonial grounds were on the far south side of the village. Will could see the huge enclosure that represented the bear's cave.

"That cave is at least 150 feet across," Will exclaimed in awe. "It's huge! It must have taken your people a long time to build it."

They had a fairly good view of the dancers down inside and could hear the beating of the drums and other instruments that were being played. The voices of the singers floated on the breeze and seemed to fill the whole sky. Even though Will was expecting it to be something very different from what he had ever seen, he stood frozen in place as he listened in amazement and watched the scene spread below him.

"Come, we must hurry," said Peteetneet as he started down the trail that led to the village. Snapped out of his trance, Will followed behind him. When the boys reached the edge of the village, they turned up the path and went to the tepee of Peteetneet's mother. Will waited outside the door while Peteetneet went inside. A minute later, the flap opened, and Peteetneet stepped back out with his mother and Tabiona. Will opened the knapsack he was carrying and carefully lifted out the currant pie his mother had given him to give to Peteetneet's mother. He blushed as he held the pie out to her and said, "A gift for you, the mother of my friend." He looked anxiously at Peteetneet to see if he had said the right thing. The Indian boy gave a tiny nod and a quick little smile. He then translated Will's message to her. Relieved, Will smiled at Peteetneet's mother as she took the gift from him.

Obviously pleased, she gave Will a big grin and said in the Ute-ah tongue, "White boy honors Light Wing with this gift." Peteetneet translated her thanks back to Will. Still smiling, she turned and carefully took the pie back into the teepee.

Tabiona looked at Will and said, "Little Bear know how to make friend. Our mother very pleased!"

Will blushed again and reached down into the knapsack and brought out the honey candy that was tied in the bright square of calico material. He reached for Tabiona's hand and pressed the package into her palm. She looked down in surprise.

"This gift is for you," Will said. "It tastes really good, and I thought maybe you would like it. I want to give you something to let you know I am very happy with the gift of moccasins you gave to me."

After admiring the bright piece of material, she carefully untied the knot and tentatively stuck one of the pieces of candy in her mouth. "Oh!" she squealed as she sucked on the chewy, golden piece.

Will beamed with pride. By the look on her face, he

knew Tabiona loved his gift. Feeling very content, he closed his knapsack and threw it over his shoulder. He turned to say something to Peteetneet when suddenly his eyes caught a light movement behind a tepee several yards away. A funny feeling in the pit of his stomach told Will that something was not right.

Just then Peteetneet turned to him, "Come now, Little Bear, we go watch dancers," he said and started to walk away. Tabiona flashed Will another big smile, and Will turned to follow Peteetneet. As he started to move he glanced once more at the tepee where he had seen the movement. Will's eyes met the sullen eyes of Squash Head and he stopped in mid-stride. Why is he looking at me that way, he thought with some dismay. I wonder if he watched me give my gifts?

Just then Squash Head spun around and disappeared behind the tepee.

CHAPTER 12

The Bear Ceremony

Will leaned against the timbers of the bear cave where he stood with Peteetneet watching the sacred ceremony. He felt very honored to be allowed inside to watch.

"We believe bear is wisest of animals and bravest of all, except mountain lion," said Peteetneet to Will. "As Grandfather told you, bear has much great magical power and aware of his brother, the *Ute-ah*. Our ceremony strengthens friendship between us."

On one end of the enclosure was a platform where the musicians played their instruments. Right next to it, a concave hole was dug into the earth—simulating a cave. Over the hole, a box or drum with an open bottom was arranged.

"Do you hear the way music sounds, Will?" asked Peteetneet. "Loud echo is sound of thunder and awake sleeping bear in mountain cave."

The dancers stopped, and the women all walked toward the men. Each one walked to a different man and picked him to dance.

"*Yi-yi!*"

Will quickly looked in the direction of the piercing sound. One of the braves was being soundly whipped with a willow stick by another man.

"Why is he doing that?!" Will whispered to Peteetneet.

Peteetneet answered, "Dance is performed by men and women together, and women must always invite men to dance. Very wrong for brave to refuse any woman who choose him to dance. It is great insult and not acceptable. Dance leader, who is usually medicine man or one of our tribal elders, punish anyone who is slow in accepting woman's dance request."

Just then, Tabiona walked over to Will and held her hand out to him. A look of panic came into Will's eyes. "What do I do, Peteetneet? I don't know how to dance!" he hissed out of the side of his mouth hoping only Peteetneet would hear.

Peteetneet laughed aloud. Tabiona looked down and blushed. She started to giggle, and Will just flat out didn't know what to do.

"Go," said Peteetneet, "Tabiona teach you. Dance not hard."

Shyly, Will walked with Tabiona to the middle of the enclosure. The men and women lined up in two long rows facing each other. Everyone was very disciplined and serious about their participation in the dance. The musicians and singers began their chanting. Following the slow beat of the drum, the dancers took three steps forward and three steps backward. Will quickly figured out what he was supposed to do. He looked over at Tabiona, and she smiled encouragingly at him. The dance became hypnotic. Besides the drum beat there was a rasping rhythm coming from the *morache,* or "bear growler," as Peteetneet called it. Tabiona called them "singing sticks." Their rasping sound was made by drawing a hard stick across the jaw-bone of a large animal. The stick player would place one end of the bear growler on his lap, with the other end leaning against the drum box. The drum box amplified the sound. It reminded Will of the clickedy-clacking sounds he used to make when he and his friends would run down the sidewalk dragging a stout stick across the slats of the wooden fences in front of all the homes down his street.

The dance went on and on. The steady beat of the drum seemed to vibrate right through Will's body and into his very bones. Will looked around him and could sense how important this ceremony was to these peo-ple. The closest thing he could compare this too was when his Ma and Pa read to him out of the Bible and taught him about God. I wonder if this is their way of feeling close to the Great Spirit, Will thought.

It was interesting to Will how the songs changed. Sometimes only the musicians chanted, and other times when the song seemed familiar, all the other men would join in.

Suddenly the music stopped. Will almost tripped

trying to stop himself from taking the next step forward. Two dancers dressed as a male and female bear sprang into the circle, pawing and prancing to symbolize that the prayers have been heard and the earth is awakened.

Tabiona smiled again at Will. "White boy learn quick. Much good dancer!" she said with approval as they walked back to the side where Peteetneet was watching them.

The sun was now straight up in the sky and shining directly down on the people within the bear cave. The singers and musicians walked over to where the tribal leaders were sitting and thanked them for the honor of allowing them to sing and play the sacred music. On the first day of the ceremony a new chief had been chosen to lead the clan. Chief Arapeen now stood up and acknowledged the thanks of the musicians.

A great cheer rose among the people and amidst the laughter and talking, all the people began to exit the bear cave enclosure. This conclusion signified the bears were awake, well fed and had found their mates. It was now time to celebrate with feasting and games!

The excitement was contagious. Will and Peteetneet jumped up and headed for the exit from the ceremonial bear cave. Food was being put out and neither boy wanted to miss out on his share. Hungry people eagerly crowded each other in their haste to get to the feast. The ceremony had lasted a long time, and it was now time to celebrate.

Will felt someone tap him on his back. He spun around to see a grinning Squash Head. "White boy learn Indian dance much good. Maybe boy like watch braves horse race after eat," he said.

Surprised, Will stuttered as he answered, "Well, yes I would." He looked over at Peteetneet to see what this was all about. Peteetneet raised his eyebrows and shrugged his shoulders. He seemed as surprised as Will did at Squash Head's friendly invitation.

CHAPTER 13

The Feast

OOOhhh, my stomach hurts," Will groaned and folded his arms across his mid-section. "I ate too much!"

"Much good food!" Peteetneet said, smiling and rubbing his hands across his own stomach. The boys hadn't wasted a single minute getting their share of the food. They had built up an appetite watching the bear ceremony, and when they came out of the enclosure and smelled the delicious aromas coming from the deer, elk and rabbit stews, they didn't hesitate for a single moment to dig into the cooking pots for their share. Besides the stews, there was an assortment of corn and nut cakes, dried fish, buffalo and an array of fruits and smashed berry sweets.

"This reminds me of when we have our Christmas dinner," Will said. "I always eat too much!"

"Christmas?" Peteetneet said in a puzzled voice. Just as Will was about to explain what Christmas meant he heard someone call out to him.

"Hey, white boy, you come watch games now."

Will looked up and saw Squash Head waving him over to where other boys and girls were gathered together by the river.

"Come, we go now," said Peteetneet. He and Will ran over to join the other young people. When they reached the river, Will smiled shyly at those nearest him. Many of them grinned acceptance back to him.

"We wait for riders to line up for race," said Peteetneet. "Our people love games and racing. Foot race almost as good as horse race."

"Hey, I like to run! Can we join in the foot races?" Will asked.

"Yes! Much fun to see white boy run with the people," Peteetneet said. "Indian children start very young to be good runner. They practice many time. Run very long way and for very long time. Great honor to be best runner in tribe. When Indian grow big enough to own horse he then give all attention to help horse be best and fastest one in tribe."

"My father told me that your people have some of the finest, well-trained horses in the West. Many people trade with the Utes for your horses," said Will.

Peteetneet beamed with pleasure. "Yes, *Ute-ah* very good with horse. Also, many other Indian trade with *Ute-ah* people for our horses," he said. "Good horse is very important. If he think he has fastest horse in village, Indian bet all he owns and all his squaw owns on a single race. To own many things not important but to have many fine horses make warrior rich and important."

"When will you have the foot races?" Will asked.

"The younger children will have foot race later in day," he said. "Come now, horses lined up and ready to go."

The two boys joined Squash Head and his friends at the side of the race track. There was an electric excitement in the air. Each family had a father or son racing, and many had made bets on the outcome.

Will and Peteetneet pushed through the throng to get a good view by the side of the track. As Will watched the men line up with their horses he noticed the track was only about the length of a city block back home.

"The horses don't race very far," he said to Peteetneet.

"*Ute-ah* horse very fast in short race," he replied to Will. "Best way to tell which is fastest horse."

Each of the men raced bareback with the rider using only a braided leather rope for a bridle. The medicine man raised a staff in the air. The men held their mounts back as each one pranced around ready to take off. It was as if the horses knew what was expected of them and were eager to run.

"*Yii hii!*" called out the medicine man as he lowered his staff to the ground with a bang. The horses exploded off the starting line, and the race was on. Will jumped up and shouted with the rest of the spectators. Horses and riders were only inches apart as they ran through the clouds of dust, and several of the riders ran into each other in their zeal to reach the finish line. A young warrior on a brown and white pinto tore over the finish line just inches before a shaggy, black mustang next to him hit the line. The winning brave threw his arms into the air, tossed his head of shiny black hair around and let out a resounding yell of triumph. The crowd shouted with him.

Squash Head gave Will a big thump on his back, nearly knocking Will right off his feet. "How you like that, white boy?" he exclaimed.

Will grinned up at the Indian, "I reckon that was just about the most exciting horse race I've ever seen!" he said.

"Now we go to shooting contest," he said to Will. "You show Indian how good white boy is with weapon. We use bow, knife and axe."

Will shrugged. "Okay," he said. He gave Squash Head a tentative smile and started to follow the older boy to the next competition.

I guess Squash Head isn't mad at me anymore, Will thought. Ah shucks, why should he be? I didn't do anything wrong. I gotta quit lettin' my imagination make somethin' outta nothin'. Will squared his shoulders and eagerly went on to the next game.

The men started to set up targets, and Squash Head walked over to Will. He had a scrap of leather and a piece of charcoal in his hands.

"White boy," he said.

Will interrupted him, "The name's Will. My friends call me Will," he said boldly to the Indian.

"White boy," Squash Head replied with emphasis, "you show Indians how white man make his language talk on skin. Put your name and your father name on skin," he said while handing Will the piece of charcoal and leather.

"You want me to write my name?" Will questioned. Squash Head nodded in the affirmative.

Will eagerly took the skin and laid it carefully on the ground. Maybe he will respect me for this, he thought. After all, I'll bet he doesn't know how to write his language.

"We don't make pictures like your people do," Will said. "We write letters that make words, so we can communicate with each other over long distances."

He first wrote his name, "This says William." Then wrote his father's name. "This says Robert, which is my father's name." He proudly held the leather up for all to see. Squash Head took the skin away from Will and with a grunt of satisfaction abruptly spun around and walked away. Will looked after him in surprise. I don't think I'll ever figure him out, he thought as he watched Squash Head walk through the crowd of people.

CHAPTER 14

Sent To The Devil

Twang!" The rock Peteetneet flung from his sling hit smack in the middle of the knot on the large pine tree that was being used as a target for this competition.

"Good shot!" Will shouted as his friend hit the bull's eye for the third time in a row. "No wonder you kill the most rabbits!" he was impressed with Peteetneet's expertise.

With a look of great satisfaction, Peteetneet jumped around in a circle while others congratulated him on his good marksmanship.

Will picked up his own sling and concentrated on putting just the right size rock into the pocket. He bounced it a little bit measuring the weight. This should work, he thought. He looked up and started to walk to the line in the dirt where each competitor stood when it was his turn to compete. A loud voice distracted him, and he turned around to see what the commotion was all about.

"*Cah ahs't te wa,*" yelled Squash Head while pointing an accusing finger in Will's direction. Surprised, Will looked up at the Indian.

"Whaaat?" he said. Puzzled and concerned, he looked all around him to see what Squash Head was pointing at.

"*Cah ahs't te wa,*" he yelled again, only louder. Suddenly, the other boys around him started to back away from Will. Fear began to show in their eyes. Some shook their heads and began saying angry words that Will could not understand. Something was very wrong. A nervous flutter began in the pit of Will's stomach.

"What's the matter?" Will demanded of Peteetneet, apprehension and concern tightening his voice.

Squash Head was talking very rapidly now, pointing his finger and throwing his arm in Will's direction. An angry murmur began to come from the crowd of people that were listening to Squash Head's words.

Peteetneet suddenly threw up his own arms, "*Mwe gah nip e gah,* (you are crazy!)" he hollered back at Squash Head. A chill ran down Will's back. He had never seen Peteetneet angry before. Something was definitely wrong here. Will grabbed Peteetneet by an arm and searched for an answer in the eyes of his friend.

"What's wrong?" he demanded.

A wave of angry frustration crossed Peteetneet's

features. "Squash Head has told *Ute-ah* people that marks you make on leather are magic only white man can do. He has told my people that in one of white man's secret meetings you write down names of our Chief and his brother, my father, and then send them to devil. That is why they died and never came back."

Will's eyes grew large with disbelief. "That's not true!" he exclaimed. "That's stupid superstitious stuff. How could they believe that?!"

Will spun around and looked at the people. They were shrinking away from him and fear was written all over their features. Suddenly, the possible danger of this situation hit Will, and he realized he'd better come up with something quick.

"*Pah u quah I,*" another loud voice rang out through the group. Everyone turned around and saw Yellow Jacket standing behind them with his arms folded firmly across his chest. A stern look was chiseled on his face.

"You like coyotes gathered around a sheep all ready to eat it up. This brave white boy come here all alone to show friendship to one of our people. He wants peace as Indian does. White boy also guest of medicine man, who welcome him as does Great Spirit welcome him during this sacred time. He chosen by our friend the bear, and it be bad medicine to any *Utay* who dares harm him."

Will was stunned by these comments. Not only had Yellow Jacket intervened in his behalf for the second time, but now he was telling the people that somehow Will was special. What in tarnation did he mean?

Suddenly, a strange thing happened. First one and then another of the villagers turned their back to Squash Head. Squash Head began to mutter angry words beneath his breath, but the people ignored him and before long every person there had his back turned to the Indian.

Yellow Jacket turned to the boys. "Peteetneet, Little Bear and Squash Head go to top of big hill on side of village. Yellow Jacket meet you there." Before anyone could comment he turned around and started walking toward the hill that overlooked the Ute village.

CHAPTER 15

A Sad Telling

I'm not going," Will said. His face was red and very angry. "I don't want to be anywhere around that idiot Squash Head. I'm sick of him."

"White boy must come!" Peteetneet said very surprised at Will's outburst. "Not disobey Grandfather. Very bad medicine!"

Grudgingly, Will started walking next to Peteetneet. "Stupid savage," he muttered under his breath. "I hate him."

They walked quickly through the village and started up the hill on the north side of the tepees. The walking took some of the anger out of Will.

"Why did they do that?" Will whispered to Peteetneet as they hurried after Grandfather.

"Do what?" Peteetneet asked.

"You know, turn their backs on Squash Head," he

said.

"When Indian see something bad happen to person he not talk about it," Peteetneet said. "If possible he stop it. If not, he turn his back, and that way he can never speak of it again. When Grandfather tell people Great Spirit welcome Little Bear, the people must listen. They not listen to Squash Head anymore."

Will breathed a sigh of relief. "Well, that takes care of the people, but I don't think Squash Head went along with the rest of them," he said.

Grandfather was standing at the top of the hill and staring out across the mountains when the boys reached the top and walked up to him. Squash Head was only a minute behind the two boys, but he went to the other side of Grandfather and stood as far away from Will and Peteetneet as he possibly could.

Ignoring the tension between the boys, Grandfather said, "Now I make you a telling ." He reached down to the pouch hanging at his waist and opened it. Drawing out a rolled up piece of tan leather, he carefully opened it up and smoothed it out on a flat rock in front of him. Curiously, the boys leaned towards the rock to see what was on the thin piece of hide. It was a pictograph story.

"During last Falling Leaf Moon," Grandfather began, "Chief Standing Bear and Chief's brother, Wa-Yo-Shaw, go on journey to find meat for village. There is plenty meat close by village, but hunting on this land belong to other *Ute-ah* clans. Our warriors respect hunting grounds of other clans, so Chief and brother go north. They go to place where much deer and elk belong to their own clan. Every clan know place of own hunting ground. Grandfather know place Peteetneet and Squash Heads fathers go to find meat. Fathers never come back, but Wa-Yo-Shaw hide telling message in hole of tree. *Ute-ah* braves find this telling when they go search for missing fathers."

Will looked at Peteetneet and then Squash Head. "Don't tell me you two are cousins!" he said.

Ignoring Will's comment, Yellow Jacket smoothed out the piece of leather and began to interpret the picture-message that was drawn there:

Two brothers, one of them a chief, by the names of

Chief Standing Bear and Wa-Yo-Shaw, took their bow and arrows and left their tepees during the Falling Leaf moon.

They traveled through the forest until they came to a river. They caught some fish to eat. They rested two days and camped that evening. At sunrise they obtained a canoe and crossed the river.

They traveled for two more days. The brothers could hear a man with a big voice. The brothers ran to see and found a man with a gun. The man ran away from the two brothers.

By a tree the two brothers discover a wounded bear. He has a sad heart. This is bad spirit medicine. The two brothers talk together. They are afraid. The brothers get their weapons and kill the wounded bear. Two brothers grieve for the dead bear. They fear the man with a gun.

The brothers send a signal fire back to their village.

"When lookout see signal from chief and his brother, he get many braves to look for them. *Utay* braves find nothing except dead bear and Wa-Yo-Shaw's hunting knife by side of dead bear. This has grieved me much," said Grandfather.

The three boys looked at the medicine man. They sensed his sorrow and did not know what to say. The hurt in Grandfather's eyes was very strong.

"I have decided that it is time for me to *pike-way* (to die)," Grandfather said to the boys. "I very old now and my usefulness to tribe is small. But before I free to go to meet Creator, must journey to death place of chief and his brother. I fear their deaths were caused by great evil. This evil chains their spirits to that place. Must find out why. Medicine man's duty to set free spirits of his own sons before he can travel to Happy Hunting Grounds. Great Spirit tell me I must take you Peteetneet, Squash Head and Little Bear on journey. Need all of you to right great wrong that has been done."

Peteetneet looked stricken, "No, Grandfather, you cannot die! You are not too old!" he said.

Squash Head just looked angry and said, "You cannot take white boy on sacred journey, Grandfather! That is bad medicine!"

Will was speechless. He didn't know what to think of what he had just heard. Even if he wanted to go, how in tarnation would he be able to talk his parents into letting him go?

Grandfather looked at the boys and said, "Great Spirit does not tell Grandfather why he must do what he must do. Grandfather listen and obey. In time all will be made known."

CHAPTER 16

The Journey Begins

Alight breeze blew on Will's face. It cooled him off and helped him to relax. He took a deep breath and looked back at the glistening waters tumbling over the boulders to the river below. Glancing up at his father, he still found it hard to believe that Pa had actually given him permission to go on this journey with Peteetneet and his grandfather. Of course the fact that Yellow Jacket and Peteetneet had accompanied Will home and politely asked Will's parents to allow him to go with them certainly helped. Will's father told him later that he had a good feeling about the medicine man, and he was sure the experience would help Will to grow and learn. Ma hadn't been so eager to let him go, but as usual she finally went along with Pa.

Will and his father got up before the sun came up and packed for the trip. They stuffed his knapsack with a change of clothing and trail food. Pa then helped him make his bedroll out of two thick wool blankets and showed him how to roll them tightly. They secured the bedroll to the back of his knapsack. Will slung it over his shoulders, and adjusted the weight so it would be comfortable to carry. He checked to be sure he had his piece of flint and steel for making fire. Then he attached his small hunting knife on the belt around his waist.

Golden spears of sunlight tipped the tops of the pine trees as Will, Tag and Pa left to meet Peteetneet at the bottom of the waterfall.

They reached the bottom of the falls and crossed beneath the shimmering curtain of water to the other side. Will took the lead and picked his way down through the boulders. He wanted to show his father where he and Peteetneet always met each other. Tag scampered along in front of them, investigating whatever critter or burrow happened to be in his path. When they reached the cool stand of cottonwood trees, Will sat down on a rock next to the little hole where he left messages to his friend. Peteetneet wasn't there yet.

"This is where Pete first cooked me a rabbit," he said to his Pa. His father looked around at the cool bower, "I can see why you like this place," he said. Sitting down on a rock across from Will, he looked at him for a moment and then said, "Will, this trip will be different from anything you have ever done before. You must remember you are the guest of these people. I gathered that it was a great honor for Yellow Jacket to include you on this journey. Their culture is very different than ours, but your friendship with Peteetneet has taught you to love and accept them for who they are. Remember, they have also had to learn to love and accept you. We are as different from them as they are from us."

"I know that, Pa," Will said.

His father studied the boy for a moment. "You must be careful with Squash Head and not let him get you angry. He will try to do that. Often when you make a friend out of an enemy he will be a friend for life. As hard as that sounds to do, you might consider it."

Just then Peteetneet appeared out of the trees. Will's pa stood up and smiled at the Indian. "Well, I'd better be goin' now," he said to the boys.

Will jumped up and gave his pa a quick hug. "Thanks, Pa," he said, "I'll do you proud, I promise!"

Will and Peteetneet watched as Will's father turned and started to make his way back through the strewn boulders and up to the path beneath the waterfall.

"We go now. Grandfather waiting," Peteetneet said to Will, then turned to walk on the path toward the village.

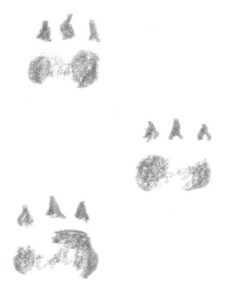

CHAPTER 17

The Wild Man

Will groaned and rolled over trying to find a more comfortable position. "What is that sharp thing poking in my back?" he wondered. Irritated, he tried to brush it away. His fingers explored underneath the blanket only to find hard dirt and a sharp rock that jabbed into his palm. He opened his eyes and suddenly things became very clear. This was not his bed! Looking around at the wet dew covering his bedroll, memories of yesterday's long, hard trek came flooding back. "Oh please, it can't be morning yet," he moaned.

With awareness came the recall of trying to keep up with the three Indians. Will had always worked hard helping his father with the stock and keeping up the place but never in his life could he have imagined the stamina of the red man. Walking or running made no difference to them. They could do either for hours on end and never even be winded. Will hadn't wanted Peteetneet, and especially Squash Head, to think that he couldn't keep up. He endured the grueling pace all day, until finally after a short and quick meal he dropped gratefully into his bedroll and fell asleep before his eyes even had time to close. If it hadn't been for the few rest stops ordered by Yellow Jacket, Will knew he would be lying half dead somewhere back on the trail.

Stretching for a moment, he listened to the fresh sounds of morning. A whippoorwill was cheerfully announcing the rising of the sun, and somewhere a frog added his deep voice to the humming of early morning mosquitoes. The sound of water trickling in a nearby stream suddenly convinced Will he'd better get up and heed the call of Mother Nature! He sat up and reached for his boots. After pulling them on he slowly stood and, while trying to stretch the stiff muscles in his calves, quickly rolled up the bedroll. He noticed the others were up and appeared ready to leave.

Peteetneet walked over to Will, "White boy get plenty sleep!" he said with a teasing smile.

"Ah shucks, Pete," Will said, "I don't think you even know how to sleep! The sun is barely coming up!"

"Grandfather say, let Little Bear sleep. He not used

to long journey like red man," said Peteetneet, "Now you ready go?"

"I'll just show you how ready I am!" Will said squaring his shoulders and throwing his knapsack over his back. "Ohhhh," he groaned as he started to walk, his legs quivering like a humming birds wing's. Grandfather raised his eyebrows to Will, but Will just gave him a big grin, turned his back to him and followed the same trail Squash Head had already left on. I'm gonna go home crippled, he thought to himself, but I'm not gonna let them see me quit!

"Tag, where are you?" he called out to his dog. Half a minute later the animal was walking next to Will, and they were on their way. Will reached into his pocket and took out a piece of the deer jerky his Pa had given him. The long trek from the day before had definitely built up his appetite. "Thank goodness I got some a this here dried meat," he grumbled to himself. He tore off a big hunk with his teeth and started chewing on it. Obviously, the Indians had eaten their breakfast while Will was still sleeping.

As the morning wore on, Will noticed the trail they were on never wandered far from the sounds of the river. "Too bad we're not going the other way," he thought. "Then we could go in the canoes. Hey! Maybe we'll come back by canoe." The thought brightened him up somewhat.

It was a warm, sunny day. The sun hadn't gotten very high before Will felt sweat trickling down the small of his back. It was going to be another grueling trek. Actually, the walking seemed to make the stiffness in his muscles feel better. Will tried to spark up a conversation with the others, but the three never spoke much as Grandfather was very eager to reach their destination. Besides that, Squash Head had made darn well sure he wasn't anywhere near enough to Will where he might have to speak to him. Things weren't any better between them, and Will tried not to think about what might happen if they happened to be put into a touchy situation together.

Suddenly Grandfather stopped and bent down to study something on the ground. The others followed to look while Grandfather pointed in several different directions with a stick.

"Many bear track," he said. "We in bear territory. Must be careful. Bear attack if he think we try to take his kill." He studied the tracks a bit more and said, "Look, she-bear with little one go through here not long ago. Track very fresh." With the tip of his finger, he gently poked at the edges of the tracks. The dirt crumbled easily into the deep impressions the animals' feet had left.

Suddenly, and without warning, a huge crashing noise sounded in the bushes next to the group. Startled, all four of them stood up and stared in the direction of the noise. Within seconds, the sound got louder, and a little snow-white bear cub came crashing through the thick branches. It skidded to a halt right in the middle of the group. Instinctively, the humans all jumped out of the little bear's path.

"*Shut t che-gah que auget* (white bear)," Grandfather exclaimed! In confusion Will looked at the others. The

Indian boys seemed just as stunned as Grandfather. Before any of them could recover from their surprise, another loud noise came from the bushes the little bear had just appeared from. In one motion, all of them spun around just in time to see a huge man explode from the same bush the little bear had come from. He was hairy and wild looking. He had a rifle in one hand and a big knife clutched in the grip of the other, and it was evident the little white bear was his prey.

CHAPTER 18

The Lost Battle

Each of them froze as they looked at the shocking figure leaping towards them. Will saw the biggest man he had ever seen. His weight did not slow the powerful man. He had a full beard that straggled half way down his chest and was dressed in dirty rough-cut skins made from the hides of deer and other wild game. He wore high moccasins similar to the kind the Indians wore. Will wondered if he were looking at a creature half-man, half-animal.

As the man leaped from the bushes and noticed the four people in front of him, he let out an angry yell. Unfortunately, Peteetneet was directly in his path. The wild man crashed into the Indian so hard he did a complete somersault right over the top of the boy. Peteetneet was thrown sideways and caught his right leg in the crack of a fallen stump. As he fell hard to the ground, his leg twisted backwards, and giving way to the unnatural pressure put on the limb, it snapped.

"Yeeeow!" Peteetneet screamed with a sharp cry of pain.

Yellow Jacket let out a small cry and turned to help his grandson. Just seconds after Peteetneet fell, Squash Head screamed and bravely dove to the ground to grab the wild man's legs. Like an irritated horse swatting at an annoying fly, the trapper reached down and with the butt of his rifle hit Squash Head square on the jaw and knocked the boy out cold.

"No! Stop!" shouted Yellow Jacket and jumped up. But the trapper was fast and before Grandfather even realized what had happened, he lifted the frail Yuta by the front of his leather jerkin and tossed the old man out of his way. Yellow Jacket crumbled into a lifeless heap on the ground.

Will hadn't been able to move. But seeing the old man lying lifeless now moved him to action. Not sure what he would do with it, Will pulled his small hunting knife out of the leather sheath hanging at his waist. The trapper, seeing the knife, threw his head back and roared with laughter. "Okay, boy, come get me with that little pig sticker," he said.

The trapper grabbed the puny knife with his thick, hard hands and threw it into the bushes. "Ouch! You're hurting me!" Will shouted as the wild man twisted Will's arms behind his back. The man reached for an old stringy piece of leather he had hanging out of a pouch over his shoulder and roughly tied Will's hands together.

"You stupid Indians," he jeered as he dragged Will over to an aspen tree and forced him to sit down. With a yell, he grabbed his rifle and ran off into the bushes in the direction the white cub had taken.

CHAPTER 19

The Bear Claw Necklace

H e's a white man!" hissed Squash Head, "Did you see that? He's a white man!" "Just shut up!" Will said, exasperated at Squash Head's hatred of the white man. He was afraid. They all were afraid, and Will knew it. He tried to ignore Squash Head. Besides, it was not hard to understand the Indian's anger. Squash Head, himself, had the beginnings of a big, ugly bruise covering most of his left cheek and jaw. He was lying on the ground, and it appeared he was too dizzy to get up and do anything.

Will looked around at the others. Yellow Jacket's eyes were half closed, and his skin had a funny gray pallor to it. That can't mean anything good, he thought. Will looked over to Peteetneet.

"Pete, are you all right?" he whispered, afraid to talk loud in case the trapper might be near by. Peteetneet slowly lifted his head and looked into Will's face. Will could see the glassy look of pain in his friend's eyes.

"Little Bear must help. Grandfather is very bad," Peteetneet said, evidently more worried about Yellow Jacket than himself.

"It's okay, Pete, don't worry, I'll think of something," Will said just to comfort his friend. Every part of his body ached. It seemed like a bad dream. How the heck am I going to help us? he thought in a panic. Secretly he wished his pa were here right now. He would know what to do. For the last little while he felt like there was something important he needed to remember. The thought kept nagging at him. What was it?

"Well, I'll be hogtied!" he said out loud, as a memory came flooding back. It was a month or so ago when he was back in the meadow throwing balls to Tag. To his amazement his pup had found a little white bear cub and started playing with him and chasing him around the meadow. Will had never even been close to a little cub before, let alone a white one with pink eyes. And now, here was another little white bear!

"Wait a minute," he wondered aloud, distracted for a moment, "Could this be the same little white cub?" The cub's appearance had come so abruptly that Will hadn't noticed the color of his eyes.

Suddenly he remembered the reason he had even met Peteetneet. The Indian had saved his life when the mother bear came looking for her baby! "Oh my heck! Oh no!" he said. "The little white cub ran through here—where in tarnation is the mother bear? She's sure to be close behind! If she finds us, she will kill us!"

"Listen!" he whispered. There was another noise coming from the bushes. Will's heart started pounding, and he clenched his hands into tight little balls. " This could be very ugly!" he said in a panic.

The noise got louder and closer. Will frantically tore at the knots in the leather strip that bound his wrists. "Tag!" he called, his voice filled with alarm. "Where are you?"

Suddenly, the big trapper came crashing again through the bushes into the little clearing. He was dragging a small doe he had evidently shot.

"Oh!" Will instantly breathed a sigh of relief when he realized it was not the mother bear. Just as quickly he tensed up, wondering what the trapper was up to this time. Now he hoped his pup hadn't heard him call.

The trapper put the doe down in the middle of the clearing. Ignoring the boys and their old grandfather, he removed the heavy leather shirt he was wearing and pulled out his big knife. Around the man's neck was a beautiful, ornate necklace made out of bear claws, eagle feathers and hare bones. A necklace that only a chief had the honor or right to wear. Grandfather and the boys all noticed the necklace at the same time. Yellow Jacket let out a moan of deep sorrow. Squash Head threw his head back and let out a long and loud howl of grief. Peteetneet hung his head and whispered hoarsely to Will, "It is necklace of chief, Standing Bear. Never would he let another man wear sacred necklace."

"No!" Will whispered back. He knew Pete was telling him that the only way the trapper would have the necklace was if he had killed the two brothers.

"Shut up!" growled the trapper. He was busy cutting pieces of meat off the small deer and didn't realize what they were all staring at. He stood up with a large chunk of meat in his hand and saw their eyes on the necklace. He threw his head back and let out a cruel, loud laugh.

"Oh, I see ya knew the two savages I got this here trophy from," he said pointing to the intricate beading on the necklace. "They got what they deserved right here on this very spot. Those two lazy red men tried to stop me from killin' a big black bear who had two of the nicest little twin cubs I ever did see. I needed 'em more than she did," he growled, the anger in his voice deepening. "You four jist scared away a rare white cub and if'n I don't git him back, you'll face the same fate of those other savages."

The boys were silent and watched the man as he took chunks of the deer and strategically placed the raw meat around the clearing and by the boys.

"This here juicy red meat will bring that little cub right back here where I kin get him." He stood up and wiped the sweat off his forehead. Putting his hands on his hips, he demanded of Will, "What is a white boy doing with a bunch of dirty Indians? You kin come to no good hangin' around with the likes a them," he said.

Will just glared at the mean man. He looked him straight in the eye and tried to make it look like he wouldn't waste his time answering someone who so totally disgusted him. But in actuality, he was so scared he was afraid he would croak if he tried to speak.

Impatient with the boy, the trapper threw his hands up in the air and growled, "Ahh, don't answer me then. Fer as I'm concerned, yer no bettrn' the likes a them." A cunning smile turned up the corners of his thick lips. He boasted and pointed to himself. "You's all lookin' at the famous Cub Bear Butler," he said. "Yah see this here deer? She be bear bait along with the rest a yah. Yeah, that's right," he said with glee, noticing the frightened looks on the faces of Will and the others. "I have buyers that pay me big money for all the cubs I kin capture. They take 'em back to the big cities, so's folks there kin come and get a good gawk at 'em. I almost had that little white cub and it's yer fault I lost him! You know how much money I wudda got outta that little bear?" he asked, his voice getting higher with the rage he was working himself up to. "More money 'n you'll ever see in yer life and I ain't about to lose it!" he yelled. "That cub'll be back lookin' for his ma and first thing she'll do is come lookin' fer the smell a this here blood. If'n yer lucky you won't even know what hit yah when she takes yer heads off with one a her big paws!" he said and laughed cruelly.

"You can't do this!" Will said in genuine shock and surprise. How could the man be so heartless!

"Oh, I can't, can't I?" the trapper said with glee. "Tell yah what, ye jist might luck out. I wounded that old sow back yonder, and she ain't movin' too fast. Maybe she'll jist ignore the lot of yah. Or then again, maybe she'll be meaner than ever a lookin' for that youngin' a hers."

Cub Bear went over to the boys and made sure they

were all securely tied up. It looked as though grandfather had slipped into unconsciousness. The trapper gave the old Yuta a small kick in the side and decided he wasn't worth taking the time to tie up. With that he grabbed his shirt and took off laughing through the bushes resuming his search for the little white cub.

CHAPTER 20

Yellow Jacket's Wisdom

Will leaned his head back against the tree. He was hot and sticky from the effort he was making to free himself. It seemed the more he pulled on the knots holding his hands, the tighter they became. He looked up at the sun and with some surprise noted that it hadn't moved in the sky much since the last time he had looked. He figured barely an hour had passed since Cub Bear left them surrounded by the deer meat. Big, black flies were crawling over the red pieces of meat, and the busy humming noise they were making only added to the discomfort he was feeling.

Suddenly, like a dark cloud blocking out the light of the sun, the magnitude of the situation washed over Will. Sweat beads gathered on his brow and upper lip. Ever since the day he met him, Peteetneet had always been the one in charge. He had always made Will feel safe. It had seemed as though there was no problem he couldn't handle. Will glanced over at his friend and saw his head slumped down on his chest. A look of pure defeat was etched on his features. This scared Will. What in tarnation am I doing here? Will thought, fresh panic choking the breath out of his lungs. Why did we even leave Boston? What were my parents' thinking? And then aloud he whispered, "We could all be killed out here!" He hung his own head down and started an earnest prayer. "Please, God, help us get out of this. We're going to die! I don't know what to do. Help me know what to do, and I promise I will even help Squash Head," he pleaded.

"Will," said a hoarse voice. Will looked up startled. Peteetneet had his head up and in his eyes was a spark of the old determination Will had come to count on. A feeling of hope came over Will. "Are you okay?" he whispered back to his friend.

"Leg not very good," Peteetneet said, "but must not give up. Spirit Wind whispers to me and tells me this is so."

Will breathed a sigh of relief and hope. He knew his friend was in pain, but this was more like the Peteetneet he had come to know so well.

"Thank you, God or Spirit Wind, for hearing us," he said softly to himself.

"Grandfather," Peteetneet said, "Can you hear me? Are you all right?" Grandfather was lying on the ground and had not moved in some time. He slowly opened his eyes and looked over at the boys. It was apparent that he was very weak, but to the surprise of everyone, he sat up. The color of his face was very gray and ashen looking, but he smiled faintly at each of the boys.

"Do not worry about Yellow Jacket," he said sternly. "Boys know old Grandfather's time is ending. If Great Spirit take him all will be well."

"No, not time yet!" Squash Head blurted out, sorrow softening his usual gruff features.

"Grandfather's two sons, Chief Standing Bear and Wa-Yo-Shaw, die in this place of great evil." said Yellow Jacket. "We must now set their spirits free. If old Grandfather die, he will soar with his sons. All will be free of evil."

"What does this mean?" Will said softly.

Yellow Jacket looked at Will. "I will tell you a telling, so you not worry about Grandfather," he said.

"Many, many suns ago, the first Ute came up from hole in earth to view green forests and blue sky. He knew Great Spirit who live in sun. This god had many name, but they not important, because he God to all people. He God to your people. All Indians go to Happy Hunting Ground in sun after death to live forever with Great Spirit. It is good place, like earth, only better with plenty of dancing and good hunting in deep green forests. When Grandfather die, his spirit soar on the winds and go with sons to this good place. One day, you too join us in Happy Hunting Ground."

"What should we do, Grandfather?" asked Peteetneet.

Grandfather slowly reached down to his waist and lifted a small dark pouch he had hanging there. "After

Grandfather's spirit leave, you must take pouch and, when it is safe, sprinkle the medicine all over ground and bushes. Give this ground to Great Spirit and my sons be set free. I travel with them."

"We have much sadness at this telling, Grandfather," said Peteetneet. Squash Head just looked at Yellow Jacket with a stricken look on his face.

"Take comfort, my sons. When time comes all will be well," Grandfather said. He breathed a deep sigh of weariness and leaned back heavily against an aging pine.

Suddenly, a noise in the bushes silenced the group. They looked at each other and tensed. "Did you hear that?" Will whispered.

CHAPTER 21

A Mother's Fury

The noises got louder, and suddenly the little white cub burst through the bushes! He slid to a halt in the middle of the clearing, his nose alert, sniffing at the smell of the raw meat. He trotted over to one of the scattered chunks and started tearing into the food. Tag jumped up from his spot next to Will and started barking furiously. Curiously, the cub looked up as Tag came to a sliding halt next to the little bear's side. Sudden recognition lit the eyes of the two little animals.

"Arrrgh," the little cub growled and batted playfully at Tag's head. Tag fell over, jumped up and nipped at the little bear's tail.

Will was stunned. "It *is* the same cub!" he yelled as he watched the two of them romp. Before long the animals were playing tug of war with the little cub's big chunk of meat.

"ROARRRR!" A holler of rage filled the clearing, and a large black bear crashed through the bushes and stood up on her two hind legs.

She roared again when she saw and smelled the humans and the fresh deer meat all together in the same place.

Will was more afraid now than he had ever been in his life! His stomach was churning so badly he thought for sure he would throw up. He struggled fiercely with the bindings that imprisoned his hands and feet. Panic had turned to cold fear and Will was unaware of the small drops of blood spreading beneath the leather strips that held him tight. A terrible picture of the mother bear's claws reaching for him filled his imagination.

Will wasn't alone. Squash Head and Peteetneet were fighting desperately with their own bonds. Yellow Jacket was struggling to stand. Just as the bear rushed forward to attack the intruders a gun shot rang out. The bear jerked as a bullet penetrated her right shoulder. With a shudder, she fell down on all fours. She let out a hideous scream and turned in the direction of her attacker. Like a madman, Cub Bear leaped out of the bushes, gun held high and ready to shoot again.

Tag started yipping, and the little bear began mewling pitifully. The two of them turned simultaneously and ran for the bushes on the other side of the clearing.

"Booomm!" Another shot rang out, and this time the bullet grazed the bear's skull. Dazed, she turned around and in confusion tried running after her cub.

"Ah-hah!" Cub Bear roared with laughter, "those bears will never git the best a ole Cub Bear!" he said. Shouldering his rifle, he ran off in the trees following the direction the animals had taken.

A horrible feeling came over Will. What if the trapper killed Tag? He screamed as loud as he could, "Tag! Tag, you come here! Right now!!" He didn't have to call again because Tag abruptly came limping through the bushes. He whimpered painfully and hobbled over to Will. That rotten old man, he thought. Tag must have been in the way and the trapper had kicked him out of his path.

In desperation, Will looked over at Peteetneet. "We gotta get free! What do we do now?" he whispered frantically.

CHAPTER 22

Peteetneet's Courage

Peteetneet's voice was very strained, "Move close and take pouch from my waist." Will wondered what Pete was trying to do, but instead of questioning his friend, he began an awkward sliding and rolling movement to try and get close to him. Unfortunately for Will, the trapper had tied his ankles together just before he left the clearing. He and Squash Head were each trussed up like a couple of chickens headed for the butcher block. The trapper must have figured Grandfather and Peteetneet weren't worth bothering about, because he had left Grandfather lying in a heap on the ground and had only tied up Peteetneet's hands. Sharp twigs and little rocks dug into Will's arms and legs, but the effort paid off and within a couple of minutes he was sitting next to his friend.

"What should I do?" he whispered.

"Put your back to me and try to get pouch. Open and take out flint. Give to me and I work knots on your hands," Peteetneet said.

Will wiggled around and put his back as close as he could get to Peteetneet. The Indian tried to help by moving closer to Will, but he cried out in pain after putting only a little pressure on his injured leg.

"We've got to splint your leg," Will said. "You'll be able to move better if we do."

Peteetneet just grunted and concentrated on moving until Will's hands were touching the pouch. Will fumbled with the lacing that tied the pouch shut. It finally opened up, and Will was able to find the sharp piece of flint that Peteetneet used for starting fires. He held it between his fingers and then scooted around so his back was to Peteetneet's back and their hands were touching. Peteetneet took the rock and deftly started sawing on the leather straps that held Will's hands. Surprisingly, it only took a minute or two, and the bands fell off.

"Oh, yes!" Will breathed a sigh of relief as he rapidly rubbed the chaffed, torn skin of his wrists, trying to get his circulation going again. He then rolled over and took the flint from Peteetneet. Quickly he sawed off the bands on his feet, and turning back to Peteetneet, freed him as well. Then he moved over to Squash Head. When he was free, Squash Head rubbed his wrists and gave Will a slight nod of his head.

I guess that means thanks, Will thought to himself

sarcastically.

Squash Head immediately turned and broke a couple of stout branches off a nearby tree. He took them over to Peteetneet.

"Must fix leg now," he said looking at his cousin. Peteetneet acknowledged him with a slight nod and shut his lips tightly together in anticipation for what was to come.

"White boy must hold Indian down while me pull leg," Squash Head said to Will.

When Will realized Squash Head was going to set Pete's leg, he turned pale. This would hurt! His pa had done this to a man on their trek west, and his screams still rang in Will's ears.

"Little Bear must get piece of wood and put in my mouth," Peteetneet said to Will.

Will found a small chunk of wood next to the fallen log Peteetneet had tripped over. He brought it over to Peteetneet and silently handed it to him. The boy took the piece of wood and, looking up at Will said, "No worry, you hold me good, and I be okay." Will couldn't believe the faith Peteetneet had in him. He shook his head in wonder. Just six months ago he would never have believed it if someone had told him what he would be doing today.

Squash head knelt down by Peteetneet's feet and carefully laid his cousin's leg out as straight as he could.

"White boy must hold Indian's arms and body down very still," he said looking at Will.

Will watched as Peteetneet put the piece of wood in his mouth, and then upon a signal from Squash Head he laid his own body over Peteetneet's chest and held his arms in a vise-like grip. Just as he got positioned, Squash Head suddenly pulled and twisted Peteetneet's leg. With a sharp snapping sound the bone in his leg slipped back into position. Will was totally taken off guard. He grimaced when he saw the agonizing look of pain etched on Peteetneet's face. It was the look of a silent scream. His teeth bit deep into the piece of wood that filled his mouth. It dawned on Will that without the wood Pete could have bitten his tongue off. Will quickly moved his weight off of his friend's chest.

"Are you all right?" he whispered to Peteetneet, his own face ashen just imagining the pain Pete must be going through.

Peteetneet moaned but nodded in the affirmative. Squash Head also shook his head in agreement and said, "Leg now straight. Must bind up quickly." He took the two straight limbs he had gotten from a tree, and put one on either side of the broken leg. Will helped hold the sticks in place while Squash Head bound them firmly to the injured leg with some strips of leather from his pouch.

"Try to get up," Squash Head said to his cousin while lifting him by the arms. It was evident that Peteetneet was in pain, but he courageously stood on his one good leg. Will found a long, stout stick and broke it off to the height of Pete's armpit. He then took the extra shirt he had in his knapsack and wrapped it around the top of the stick to make it more comfortable on top.

"Use this as a walking stick," he said to his friend.

He put the stick under Peteetneet's armpit and adjusted it so the shirt cushioned his arm from the sharp end of the stick.

"Now try hopping and using the stick as your other leg," Will said.

Peteetneet stumbled some as he first tried the awkward movement, but he soon got the hang of it and before long was hopping around on the stick and keeping his hurt leg out of the way.

Grandfather had been quietly watching the boys take care of Peteetneet. He now spoke up, "Come, my sons," he said, "You much brave. Do work of warrior." The boys looked at each other with a mixture of surprise and pleasure on their faces. This was a supreme compliment coming from the tribal medicine man. All of them moved close to the old man to see what they could do for him. Peteetneet was obviously in pain, but it did not stop him from getting around on his stick.

"Reach into large pouch and get out medicine," Grandfather said. "It will take pain out of leg." Squash Head carefully untied a large pouch hanging on Grandfather's right side. He reached in and pulled out several little bags.

"Black bag hold leaves of spruce and birch. It make bone heal good," he said. "Later heat water for drink. Mix birch and peppermint. Will ease pain."

Peteetneet carefully sat down by the stump he had hurt his leg on. Will and Squash Head followed Yellow Knife's instructions and made a poultice out of the herbs and some rabbit fat. They then spread the poultice on Peteetneet's leg and carefully bound it with part of Will's other shirt.

They had barely finished taking care of him when they heard a noise in the distance. A man's voice came bellowing through the trees. At least it isn't the mother bear, Will thought with some relief.

"Now quick, put the bands back around your hands and feet and make it look as though you are still tied up," Will said. "If the trapper comes back and sees us free, he may kill us right away. At least this way we can make a plan for escaping."

The boys had no sooner gotten to their places, sat down and put their hands behind their backs, than the trapper came crashing through the bushes, dragging the little white cub behind him on some kind of leash.

CHAPTER 23

In Enemy Hands

Will watched wide-eyed as the trapper shoved his way through the brush and came into the clearing dragging the little white bear cub behind him.

"I ain't got no more need for the likes of you," sneered Cub Bear. "As yah kin see I got my trophy. No thanks to the lot of you almost messin' everythin' up!" he said and yanked hard on the muzzle and rope tied around the little white bear's neck. The bear moaned pitifully. Will could see he was scared and confused. He hated to think how frightened the little bear must have been when Cub Bear captured him.

A snide smile curled the corners of Cub Bear's lips, "I'm gettin' my gear outta here and you lazy, good fer nothin' mess a humanity kin jist sit here'n figger out what yer gonna do when this cub's ma gits her senses back and comes lookin' for her youngin'.' "

Will listened to the trapper and could feel the hair standing on the back of his neck. He felt the heat rising in his face, and before he realized what he was doing, he gathered the juices in his mouth and spit as hard as he could right at the trapper's face. The man's eyes widened at the spunk of the boy.

"Eeeek!" Squash Head let out a squeak of surprise. For an instant, a glint of respect shone in old Cub Bear Butler's eyes. Then he threw his head back and let out another howl of laughter.

"Spit all ye want, boy, it'll be yer last pleasure," he said and then turned his back to Will and the others and began gathering up his equipment scattered in the middle of the clearing.

It is now or never, thought Will. He looked over at Peteetneet and Squash Head. His eyes asked them a silent question. Are you ready? With a slight nod, both boys acknowledged Will's question. Will silently prayed. Their plan was simple. The trapper didn't know his prisoners were untied, and they hoped the element of surprise would give them the advantage. When his back was turned they planned on jumping him all at once. It wasn't much, but if they caught him off guard maybe they could knock him out just long enough to escape. He knew the burden of their plan would rest on himself and Squash Head. Yellow Knife and Peteetneet were too injured to be much help. He couldn't worry about that now, because this would be their one and only chance. If they didn't try to do something, their chances of escaping the fury of the mother bear were about as good as nothing.

The boys summoned up all the courage they had. Quietly they dropped the bands of leather off their wrists and feet. Peteetneet tightly gripped the big rock he held in his hand. His job was to hit the trapper in the head once Will and Squash Head jumped the big man.

Watching each other, Squash Head and Will stood up at the same time. Peteetneet slowly stood and carefully positioned himself behind the two other boys. All three of them held their breath when Cub Bear turned a bit side ways to slip his big knife in its sheath. He then turned back away from them and knelt down to the ground to stuff some rope and halters into the knapsack he carried over his left shoulder.

Will glanced sideways to make sure the other two boys were ready. Out of the corner of his eye he saw old Yellow Jacket slowly get up. It's now or never, he thought. He gave a slight wave of his hand, and he and Squash Head took two big running steps and leaped onto Cub Bear's back.

"What's this?" the trapper yelled.

He stood up with the two boys clinging to his neck, their hands yanking his hair and legs wrapped around his body. The man was powerful, and in a flash Will was thrown into the air, legs and arms flying in all directions. He found himself in a crumpled heap, lying in a small bush next to where the little white bear was tied. He looked up just in time to see Cub Bear spinning in circles while Squash Head clung onto the man for all he was worth. It reminded Will of the time he was hunting with his pa, and in answer to a terrible scream, they came around a trail in the woods just in time to see a cougar clinging to the back of a large elk. The elk was kicking and shaking for all he was worth, but the cougar just dug his claws in deeper, and no matter how hard he tried, the elk could not get rid of his enemy.

The trapper swiped at him and tried to pry the annoying boy off of his body. But Squash Head was no small person. He was tall and stocky for an Indian, and Will noticed with instant satisfaction that Cub Bear found himself having a much harder time getting rid of the Indian boy than he had Will.

Peteetneet stood just out of reach waiting for an opportunity to whack the trapper with his rock. At the same time, with a miraculous burst of energy, Yellow Jacket ran to the trapper and tried to tackle him below the knees. "Yeooow!" screamed Grandfather as Cub Bear's natural reflexes came into action and with his big foot caught Yellow Jacket hard, right in the pit of his stomach.

"No!" Will screamed when he saw Grandfather rolling on the ground in a tight ball. Suddenly, he saw Squash Head flung to the ground. Will jumped up and rushed into the massive arms of the trapper, hitting and kicking for all he was worth.

"You pot-lickin' sons of the devil!" Cub Bear screamed in a rage. "I'm gonna make ya wish you'd never been born!" At the same time, he kicked out at Peteetneet who had been trying bravely to hit the man with his rock. Unfortunately, the boy's strength was almost gone. His injured leg had taken its toll on him, and he didn't have much energy left to do any good in the fight. Cub Bear knocked Peteetneet's crutch out from under his arm, and he fell to the ground with a hard thud.

Will squirmed in the big man's arms. He tried desperately to free himself.

"Oww! Stop!" he yelled as the trapper jerked his arms behind his back and shoved them up toward his head. He held Will's arms with one hand and grabbed one of the ropes he had been putting into his knapsack. With it he trussed Will up so tightly he couldn't move his hands or arms. "Sit right there," he snapped angrily at Will while shoving him onto the ground. He took another rope and went over to Squash Head and tied him up so tight it reminded Will of a rancher getting ready to brand one of his stock. Surprisingly, he didn't tie either of the boy's feet. Next he went over to Grandfather and with his foot rolled him over.

"You've killed him!" Will cried out when he saw the blood trickling out of the corner of Yellow Jacket's mouth. His eyes were closed, and Will couldn't tell if he was breathing.

"Mwe gah cah chits! You rat!" Peteetneet moaned with great sorrow in his voice.

Will fought tears as they came unbidden to his eyes.

The trapper turned around and yanked Will up onto his feet. While holding one of Will's arms, he grabbed one of Squash Head's arms. He then took one of his halters he used to tie the bears up with and connected it from Will's neck to Squash Head's neck. He turned around to Peteetneet and said, "If'n you wanna live, ya better grab that crutch and walk in front of your friends. If'n you don't move fast enough, it won't hurt my feelin's none to leave ya here with the ole man fer bear bait." He then jerked on the rope connecting Will and Squash Head and demanded, "Get movin' now. Yer walkin' in front of me, and if ya go too slow you'll feel my foot in the seat of yer pants."

He didn't have to ask twice. Will started moving in the direction Cub Bear pointed. With one last quick look at Yellow Jacket, Will silently prayed that the old man was just unconscious and by some miracle would come to after they left. He grabbed Peteetneet's arm and helped him move along in front of him. Squash Head had no choice but to move quickly as he was tied close behind Will.

"Where are you taking us?" Will asked risking the trappers anger for an answer.

"Yer goin' to my cabin where I'll decide jist exactly what to do with the lot of you. Now shut up and git movin'," he said while dragging the reluctant little bear behind him.

CHAPTER 24

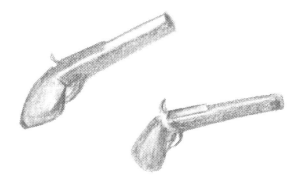

Attack In The Night

The sun had set a short while ago, and it was beginning to get dark. The three boys were sitting against the back wall of Cub Bear's cabin. From his corner, Will watched warily as the trapper staggered up and lit a couple of lanterns in the room. The big man then sat in a crude wooden chair next to the table where he was eating his supper. He lifted a flask of some kind of liquid and gulped at its contents. With a rumbling that came from the depths of his barrel chest, he let out a huge belch. He took his hand and wiped his mouth then leaned back contentedly in his chair. It appeared he had forgotten about his three prisoners.

Will looked out the small window by the big door of the cabin and noticed a tiny sliver of light coming up over the tops of a thick stand of pine trees. It was very bright and forecast the coming of a full moon. He turned his head sideways to see how the others were doing. Peteetneet had his eyes closed and his head leaned back against the rough wooden wall. Squash Head was staring at the trapper with an angry scowl pinching the features of his face. It was now easier for Will to understand where the boy's hatred of the white man came from. This trapper certainly did nothing to endear Will's people to Squash Head—especially now that it was confirmed a white man had killed his father and his uncle.

Will squirmed around trying to get himself in a more comfortable position. There were pine boughs strewn about the back of the cabin floor. It appeared as though they were used as mattress ticking for the trapper's bed and Will tried to sit on a couple of them. Unfortunately, they did not add much to his comfort.

The journey to Cub Bear's cabin had taken them close to two hours. They traveled a well used game trail through the woods when finally it broke open into a little clearing not far from the river. The cabin was hewn out of rough timber and stood about a hundred yards from the water. It was evident that no woman had helped make this place a home. The ceiling was tall, to fit the height of the big man. The door was massive and wide—obviously planned that way so the trapper could get his cages and their contents in and out with ease.

On the wall just inside the door were a half a dozen crude pegs that held extra clothing and gear. The floor was made of packed dirt. There was a stone fireplace on one end of the single room and a huge bear rug lay in front of it. There was also a big chair set in front of the fireplace. It was made out of logs and had a slightly tilted back. It had arms on the sides and was covered with another big bear skin. It looked surprisingly comfortable and was the only item in the cabin that had the appearance of luxury. The only other furniture was a big plank table that stood in the middle of the room with a simple, four-legged pine stool sitting on one end. On the table was a twin pair of 34-caliber Colt revolver pistols, loaded and ready to fire. Cub Bear was apparently ready for any surprises.

Will was nervous. A chill came over him, and he shivered. What was the big man going to do with them? The three of them had been sitting against this back wall where Cub Bear had shoved them down onto the hard floor. It had been at least an hour since the trapper had fixed himself some supper. The longer Will sat watching the man the more uneasy he became. It wasn't what the man had done to them that made Will nervous, it was what he hadn't done! Instead of talking to them and even being mad at them, he had totally ignored them. Not only had he not said anything to them, but he hadn't offered them a morsel of food or even a small drink of water. It was as though they were some of his caged animals and not worthy of his notice or conversation.

The big man abruptly got up, walked over to the cabin door and opened it. The little white cub was in a crude iron cage right outside the door. When the animal saw the man he started bawling all over again. Will winced at the fear in the little bear's voice. The poor little animal had cried miserably throughout the entire trek to the cabin. Cub Bear grinned at the animal's discomfort. "Yer gonna make me a couple a good twenty-dollar gold pieces," he said. He then picked up the cage and half-carried, half-dragged it in the door of the cabin. He set it down close to the door opening but a little off to the side where it would be out of the way.

There was only one other window in the cabin, and it was just above the three boys' heads. Will twisted around to get a better look at it. The window had an oilcloth cover that was pulled over to one side. The window let both light and fresh air come in. During cold nights the oilcloth would serve to keep the wind and rain out. Right now Will could see the sky darkening and one bright star barely beginning to twinkle in the distance.

"Hey," Will whispered to Peteetneet, "This window might be a chance for us to escape. If the man goes to sleep, maybe we could climb out this way. We'd have to be quiet, but it might be our only chance."

"Let me look," Peteetneet said. At the same time Squash Head looked up at the window.

"I tallest," said Squash Head, "when white devil sleep, Will go out window. Then I lift Peteetneet. You help him get out," Squash Head said looking at Will.

"He looks tired to me," said Will, "if we are real quiet we might just get away with it. If we don't at least try who knows what he will end up doing to us tomorrow. I know he doesn't want us to go back to your village and tell the people that he has your chief's sacred necklace, and that makes me real nervous."

"We watch now," Peteetneet said quietly and leaned back against the cabin wall. It was obvious his leg was giving him grief.

Will also leaned back against the wall, pretending to get sleepy. If the trapper looked at them he didn't want the man to suspect anything out of the ordinary. He was clever and Will knew it would be a small miracle if they pulled this off. They couldn't be too careful. As bad as Peteetneet's injury was, it was also insurance for the boys. The man probably figured they wouldn't try anything fancy, because they couldn't move quickly with Peteetneet's bad leg. If Will was guessing right, the trapper wasn't paying as much attention to the boys as he normally would.

After filling his stomach with food and having plenty to drink, Will could see the man was getting sleepy. He stood up and yawned. The food, and a day of running around the woods, was obviously catching up to him. He walked over to the lanterns and turned them down. The dying embers of a small fire in the fireplace gave a soft glow to the room.

By now even the little bear had stopped his pitiful moaning. Glancing at the bear and giving a grunt of satisfaction, Cub Bear sat down on his stool. Soon, Cub Bear's eyelids started to droop. He folded his arms on the tabletop and sleepily put his head down on top of his arms. Will almost didn't dare breathe.

"He's falling asleep!" he whispered hoarsely to his two companions. All three of them kept their eyes glued to the still form in front of them.

It seemed like an eternity, but only twenty minutes

had passed when the big man's breathing finally became heavy and even. Soon he started to snore.

Squash Head whispered, "We stand now. White boy go out window." On an unspoken cue, the two boys each took one of Peteetneet's arms and carefully stood up with him. It was awkward with their hands still tied, but fortunately, the trapper had never bothered tying their feet.

"Ohhhh," groaned the big man as he turned his head and unconsciously searched for a more comfortable position on his arms. The three boys froze. They were all standing now and none of them dared move. Please don't see us! Will thought fervently.

They stood without moving for at least five minutes. It was probably the longest five minutes of Will's life. Squash Head finally gave the signal for Will to put one of his feet into Squash Head's clasped hands so he could lift him up to the window. Just then they heard a quiet but strange noise.

"Scratch, scratch—." Again, just as if on cue, all three boys froze in place. "Screech, screech—." They all heard the slight noise coming from the front of the cabin.

"Scratch, scratch—." It came again—a noise that could only be made by sharp claws being drawn down over rough bark. This time it was louder! Suddenly, there was a low and ominous growl!

CHAPTER 25

Angry She Bear

Not good!" Peteetneet hissed, his eyes getting big with anticipation and fear. "Big animal out there!"

"Ohhhh—," moaned the trapper. The noise seemed to penetrate through the deep numbness of his sleep, but although irritating, it did not quite wake him up.

Suddenly the noise became louder, and it was at the door of the cabin. The little cub started bawling again. The huge roar of an angry bear abruptly shook the very walls of the building. Cub Bear shot up from the stool. All traces of the deep sleep he had been enjoying were instantly gone. Will could tell that for a split second the man was disoriented.

Then the door of the cabin came crashing inside, barely missing the big table as it fell to the floor. Darkening the opening was a huge black bear. It was standing up on its two back legs, and was so tall it filled the huge doorway. It was the little cub's mother. She was the embodiment of a terrible nightmare. Her front, right shoulder was bloody from a gunshot wound. Spittle dribbled down the front of her chin where long, sharp teeth gleamed in a mouth stretched wide open from her terrible roaring.

Will and the other boys stood rooted to the spot they were standing on. As Will watched, too frightened to move, it seemed as though everything was moving in slow motion. Especially his own feet!

The trapper grabbed both pistols off the table. One in each hand, he simultaneously fired the guns. The bear fell down on all four legs and let out another ear-deafening scream as both bullets ripped through her fur. She seemed to be mortally wounded, but that didn't stop her. She charged the trapper. Cub Bear stumbled backwards over his stool and grabbed for his big knife. He fell to the floor just as the she-bear reached him.

As if gone mad, he yelled out, "If'n I'm goin' down, so are you!" He lifted his arm to thrust the big knife into the black mass of fur coming down on him. But with one massive swing of her huge paw, the bear swiped the knife out of his hand. It went flying across the room and hit the back wall where the three boys were watching in shocked silence.

The loud clattering of the knife jolted the boys to action. Will didn't need any more encouragement than that. Almost faster than the blink of an eye, Will catapulted himself out the back window. He crashed to the ground and picked himself up just in time to break Peteetneet's fall as he came rolling out behind him. The boy let out a big yelp of pain as Will awkwardly tried to catch him. Both were down on the ground when Squash Head came flying out in a sprawling heap next to them.

"Let's get outta here!" Will squeaked. He grabbed one of Peteetneet's arms and started to help him up.

"Wait," Squash Head said. "Listen!" But there was nothing to listen to! Where as only moments ago Cub Bear was cursing and screaming and the she-bear was roaring, now it was dead quiet. Was the trapper dead? If so, why wasn't the mother bear making any noise? Had they killed each other?

Without a word, the boys looked at each other, questions in their eyes. At the thought of what he was about to do, Will's heart started to pound. But in spite of his fear, Will got up and as quietly as he could crept over to the edge of the window. Squash Head followed. Cautiously, they peeked over the bottom edge. It took a second for Will's eyes to adjust to the semi-darkness. But then he saw him. The trapper was lying in a heap on the floor. His body was twisted sideways, and there was blood on his chest and arms where the bear's claws had left deep scratch marks. It wasn't a pretty sight.

The boys couldn't tell if he was dead or not. But where was the bear? Neither boy could see her in the cabin. The little white cub's cage was now half out of the cabin doorway. It appeared as though the bear had tried to get it out of the cabin, but one of the iron bars had caught on the big metal latch attached to the door. It was stuck, and the little cub was still a prisoner inside.

"Let's go before we get in more trouble," Will whispered to Squash Head. But the Indian was staring at something in the cabin.

"Come on, this is our chance to get away!" Will said with more urgency.

Squash Head turned around. His face had a funny look on it that Will couldn't quite read. He began pulling at the bonds holding his hands together. The boys had loosened them earlier while waiting in the cabin and watching Cub Bear eat. Will helped him tug at the knot, and soon the ropes fell off. Each of them got their hands free and threw the rope on the ground.

Squash Head turned back to the window. "Look," he whispered and pointed at the trapper. Will looked where the boy was pointing.

Suddenly it dawned on him—the necklace! The one that had belonged to Squash Head's father. The one that was reserved only for the chief and was still hanging on the wounded body of Cub Bear. Will looked back at Squash Head.

"Your life is more important than the necklace," he hissed. When the Indian didn't answer him, Will knew Squash Head would not leave without the sacred necklace. Will turned to Peteetneet.

"Let me help you up," he whispered. "Do you think you can get to the safety of those trees over there?" he asked while pointing to a tree line about a hundred yards behind the cabin.

Peteetneet was still in a great deal of pain. Even though he refused to admit it, his face couldn't hide the agony he was feeling. When Peteetneet didn't answer him, Will said, "You can't help us Pete and you know it. If you can get yourself to the safety of those trees that will be a big help," he pleaded.

Peteetneet looked hard at Will. He didn't say anything but lifted his arm, so Will could help him stand. Will picked up the walking stick Squash Head had had the sense to throw out the window and helped Peteetneet adjust it under his armpit. As Peteetneet turned to go to the trees he said to Will, "You much good friend. I pray to Great Spirit to protect you both," he said very seriously and started to hobble away.

Will turned back to Squash Head. "Are you sure you want to do this?" he whispered, hoping the Indian had thought better of this folly.

"White boy, you go. Squash Head get necklace," he said, pointing at himself.

"No," Will stood his ground defiantly. "I don't think it's smart, but I'm not lettin' you go in there alone, even if the trapper is dead." And under his under his breath Will added, "and I sure hope he is."

Squash Head raised his eyebrows and stared at Will. He looked as though he was going to say something but shrugged instead and turned back toward the window.

"We go back this way," he said, "Mother bear may be watching cub from the front." He then lifted himself to the ledge of the window and tumbled headfirst back into the room.

Taking a deep breath and swallowing the fear that fought its way up his throat, Will followed.

CHAPTER 26

The Daring Rescue

The faint light of twilight was now gone, and only the light of the full moon illuminated the interior of the cabin. It wasn't much to see by. The boys' paused a moment for their eyes to adjust. Neither spoke. Both were staring at the still form of old Cub Bear. He had been wounded very badly, but neither of them could tell if he was actually dead or just unconscious. They stood quietly and watched to see if he made any kind of movement.

It seemed an hour, but after only a few minutes Squash Head nodded to Will and they carefully tiptoed over to the big man. He was lying on his side, and the necklace was caught underneath one arm. The other arm was flung out in front of him and on top of the fallen door. His hand was only inches from the iron cage that held the little white cub. It looked as though he had rolled over and jumped up when the bear batted the knife out of his hand. While the boys were jumping out of the back window, he must have tried to make it to the door. But it appeared that the bear caught him in flight and gave him a killing blow to the head. There was an ugly wound in the back of his skull.

Will looked over at the little white cub. He was staring at Will and surprisingly not uttering a sound.

Both boys leaned down and looked into the man's face. Each was ready to flee at the slightest sign of movement. Cub Bear's eyes were closed, and he was very still. Will couldn't tell if he was breathing. He put his hand under the man's nose, but he could feel no air coming from the nostrils.

"He not live," said Squash Head confidently. "I take necklace."

Squash Head tried to pull the necklace over the man's head, but it wouldn't budge. Cub Bear was a big and heavy man.

"Help roll him on his back," he said to Will.

Squash Head stood at the trapper's back and put both his hands on the man's shoulder. Will got on the front side of the man and when Squash Head nodded he pushed at the same time the other boy pulled. With a flopping sound, the man fell from his side onto his back. Will sucked in his breath when he saw the deep wounds the mother bear's claws had made in his chest. He looked at Squash Head, but the other boy didn't pay much attention.

Will realized this was nothing new to the Indian. His people grew up learning to deal with the fragile balance between life and death and nature. Peteetneet had taught Will early in their friendship to respect the land and the gifts nature had to give, and also that each living creature had its time and place for life or death. To live a long life one had to live in harmony with nature and be honest in one's dealings with her. This had never been more apparent to Will than at this very moment as he witnessed the consequence of Cub Bear's wanton destruction and killing of the bears in this forest.

"Lift his head," Squash Head said to Will as he lifted the heavy, ornate necklace off the man's chest. Surprisingly, the necklace had not been touched by the mother bear. Will grimaced as he lifted up the big man's head a few inches, so Squash Head could get the necklace off.

"Come now, we go fast," Squash Head said after freeing the necklace. Both boys jumped up and turned back toward the window they would again escape out of.

"Eeeeooww!" A pitiful bawling noise came from the little white cub still trapped in the cage. Will froze and spun around. He looked at the little bear, torn between what he should do. He was afraid, but if he didn't help the bear he would die in that cage. Who would get him out?

"Come now!" Squash Head urged.

"You go—I've gotta get the little cub free," Will said. Just then both boys heard a low growling noise outside the front of the cabin. It sounded like it was some distance away. Perhaps close to the river.

"You crazy, white boy! That mother bear. She be very angry!" Squash Head took a couple of running steps and jumped out through the back window.

Will hesitated. Just then the baby cub cried out

again. Will couldn't stand it. If I hurry I can set the baby free and get out the back window before the mother can get inside, Will rationalized to himself.

Will turned back towards the trapper and took two leaping steps to the iron cage. It had a simple latch on it that only needed to be sprung, but unfortunately, the latch was on the bottom side of the cage. Will knelt down. He would have to flip the cage over.

"It's okay, boy," he said to the now loudly bawling cub. He grabbed the cage and struggled to turn it over. His first try was a failure. The baby cub was heavier than he had anticipated.

"Roarrr!" The growling noise from the river had turned into a roar, and if Will was not mistaken the noise was closer than it had been before. Grunting, he heaved with all his might.

"Yes!" he yelled as the cage flipped over. Just as he grabbed the latchet to release it, something grabbed his ankle in a vise-like grip. "What?" he yelled, fear making his voice reach a higher pitch. He twisted over on his side, and to his horror he saw a wild-eyed Cub Bear struggling to say something to him.

"Let go a my foot!" Will pulled and fought against the powerful hand.

"I'm gonna—," the trapper whispered hoarsely. Will didn't catch what the man was saying. He grabbed at the big hand and tried to pry the fingers off of his ankle. Behind him the angry mother bear was getting closer. The hair was standing on the back of Will's neck. He panicked as he tried to free his leg and, at the same time, turn around to see where the mother bear was.

"Yeoweee!" Just then Squash Head leaped back through the window. He had a big stick in his hand and in two bounding steps reached the trapper and hit him over the head. The blow rendered the man unconscious, or maybe even killed him! Neither boy took the time to find out.

Will frantically pried at the fingers that were locked in a death-grip around his ankle. Squash Head bent to help him. The Indian boy was strong, and within a minute Will was free of the hand.

"Thanks," he breathed in relief.

"Come now!" Squash Head yelled at Will. "Mother bear close!"

Will looked out the door, and sure enough, the mother was struggling towards the cabin. She had been badly wounded. Her first wound came earlier in the day when Cub Bear had shot her in the shoulder. The next was in the cabin when he shot his two pistols at her. She didn't seem to have much strength left in her, but she was steadily making her way back towards the front door where her baby cub was.

"Go!" he yelled to Squash Head, "I'm right behind you!"

Believing Will really was right behind him, Squash Head turned his back and ran to the escape window. When Will saw him move he turned once more to the latchet on the iron cage trapping the little cub. It was stiff and didn't pop right open. Will looked up and saw the bear getting closer. His hands began to shake. He gripped the handle and pulled so hard he felt the blood leave his fingers. He struggled and pulled on the stubborn piece of metal.

Just then the mother bear reached the door. Only the iron cage separated her from Will. Will was so frightened he just stared at her. His legs were like two hitching posts stuck deep in the ground, and he found he couldn't move even an inch.

In one last mighty effort, the mother bear stood on her hind legs, threw back her head and roared. Will flinched. Is this it? he thought. At the same instant by some miracle, the latchet on the cage released, Will flung open the door, and the little bear ran free. The mother bear dropped to all fours and eagerly greeted the wet tongue of her little one licking her face.

Will slowly stood up, hoping she wouldn't notice him. But unfortunately, she again stood up on her two hind legs. Will didn't know whether to run or stay. Worse, his body didn't seem to be responding to his frantic thoughts of escape! His knees felt as wobbly as a new baby colt.

The mother bear lifted her head and then looked Will straight in the eyes. She didn't make a sound. Will was stunned. As he stared back at the bear he thought, This can't be—I really must be crazy!

But just as suddenly as she had stood up, she dropped to all fours and turned her full attention to her baby.

Not taking his eyes off the bear for even an instant, his legs still like mush, Will backed slowly around the still form of the trapper. He couldn't believe his luck as he inched his way to the window in the back of the room. He noticed the mother moving slower and slower as she tried to take her baby away from the cabin. She left a trail of blood behind her, and it wasn't long before Will saw her fall heavily to the ground. Will noticed the baby mewling as he licked his mother and crawled all over her. Will felt a quick twinge of sorrow for the little bear.

He then turned and did his own version of a flying leap out the back window.

CHAPTER 27

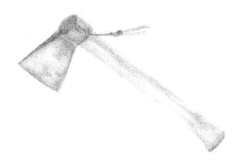

Flight At Night

Squash Head was waiting at the bottom of the window and caught Will as he came tumbling out. The Indian's eyes were big and full of surprise.

"Me saw bear," he said to Will. "She could kill you, but she thank you for helping cub!"

"What?" said Will. "Thanked me? I was just darn lucky she didn't decide to make me her supper for tonight!"

"No, Little Bear has magic with the bear," Squash Head said very seriously.

Will looked at the other boy in surprise. He had actually called him by the Indian name Peteetneet had given him. As far as he was concerned, that in itself was magic! He knew Squash Head would never do that unless he felt Will was on equal terms with him.

"Thank you for saving my life," Will said back with equal sincerity.

Squash Head shrugged. "Every day work for warrior," he said proudly. Obviously he was very pleased that Will recognized his bravery in the ordeal they had just come through.

"Little Bear brave to help Squash Head get sacred necklace," he said. "Tribal elders be much pleased." He then put the necklace over his own head for safe keeping.

Will felt really good inside. Was it only yesterday he'd felt nothing but anger and dislike towards the boy? It was unbelievable they had come through this ordeal alive. Without each of them doing their part neither would have made it. Squash Head really was brave. He had proven that by his willingness to go after something he knew was important. Will realized he had just developed a new respect for the Indian. The experience had bonded them together in such a way that he knew Squash Head would never think of him as just a "white boy" again. He couldn't help but give the other boy a big smile.

Suddenly Will remembered Peteetneet. Was he all right?

"Come, we must find Pete. I hope he made it to the trees," he said to Squash Head as he took off running for the tree line.

It only took a minute or two to reach the trees. Peteetneet must have watched them coming, because he hobbled out from behind a big pine.

"You have the necklace!" he said in awe. "Was it much trouble?"

Will and Squash Head looked at each other and

rolled their eyes.

"Ah shucks, no," Will said with a twinkle in his eye. "But how are you? Can you walk on your crutch so we can git outta here?"

"Me go where you go," Peteetneet said with a very determined look.

"Wait a minute," Will said, and he walked a short ways east of where they had been standing. The other two boys followed him to see what he was looking at.

They were on a little rise and could look down to the front of the cabin. Will wanted to see if the mother bear was still there or if she and her baby had left.

"Look," he said to his friends and pointed over by the river. The mother bear was still lying down. She wasn't moving at all, and the little cub was frantically licking and nuzzling her face.

"She didn't make it," Will whispered. "What will the little bear do?"

"Cub maybe all right," said Peteetneet, "Trust Mother Earth to take care of her own. We must go now. Grandfather back in forest!"

Will reluctantly turned away from the sorry sight of the little bear. He had risked everything to save him. Well, at least his chances were better now than they would have been if he hadn't gotten him out of that iron cage.

Peteetneet stopped in mid-stride. "What about trapper?" he said suddenly remembering the man who had been up to no good.

"Uhhh, we're actually not sure if he is alive or dead," Will said trying to answer him. "Like you said, we'll let Mother Earth decide what to do with him. Keep walking, Pete, and we'll fill you in on what happened while we try to find Grandfather."

The boys started down the same game trail Cub Bear had brought them on to get to his cabin. With the help of Squash Head, Will filled in the details of what had happened. Peteetneet stopped several times to look at the two boys to make sure they weren't joking with him.

"Great Spirit watch over you both," he said in amazement as they finished the telling.

The boys just smiled and the more Will thought about it, the happier he felt to be alive!

They continued on as best as they could. It had been a grueling day, and signs of weariness were showing on all of them. Peteetneet was in the lead. Will did not want to rush him while he was struggling so hard to walk on the makeshift crutch. He and Squash Head offered to make a travois and carry him, but he refused. "I walk," he said, very determined.

By now it was very dark, and the only thing that made it possible to walk was the full moon. "Maybe the Great Spirit is watching over us," Will mused. "I bet the Great Spirit is the same person as God." Will then whispered a little prayer. "Thank you, God, for watching over us, 'cause I know we would have never made it without you. If it's okay with you, could you give us one more little blessing and help us to find Grandfather?" he asked. When he was through, he felt a quiet peace come over him. *It's gonna be okay*, he thought and kept walking.

Suddenly, Will stopped. "Sh—Shhh!" he whispered urgently. Was it his imagination or did he hear something moving on the trail behind them?

Squash Head bumped into him. "What is it?," he asked. Peteetneet also stopped and the three of them listened intently. They didn't hear anything, and just as Will was about to start moving again, they all heard it. Only this time it was louder.

"There is something!" Peteetneet whispered. "Get off the trail and hide."

The three boys slipped into some bushes next to the game trail. Subconsciously, each one tried to hold his breath as the noise got louder and louder.

"It is animal," Squash Head said. "Be very still. Maybe it pass by. If not, I use knife to protect us."

Will gave him a funny look. I hope our escape back at the cabin doesn't make him overconfident! Will thought.

The trail was bathed in a silvery, washed-out light. It was easy to see, but there were still dark shadows around the trees and bushes. If the creature was crafty enough, it could be right on top of them before they realized it was there. The noises became louder. Besides the rustling sound of bushes being pushed aside and twigs snapping on the forest floor, they could hear low grunting noises. Noises that could only come from a fairly big animal.

The boys hunkered down and tried to make themselves as invisible as possible. Their eyes were glued to the bend in the trail behind them.

Just then, they saw the branches part on a big scrub

oak bush. Will tightly gripped the handle of a stout stick he had found and planned to use as a weapon if necessary. He was glad Squash Head had grabbed the knife out of Cub Bear's cabin before leaving. It might be their only real protection.

Suddenly, a big snow-white ball of fur came trotting straight to their hiding place.

"It's the little white bear!" Will yelled as he and Squash Head jumped up out of the bushes.

CHAPTER 28

Does He Live?

S hoo!" Will yelled, trying to chase the little white cub away. Nothing he did intimidated the little bear. He came trotting right back to Will. In frustration, Will realized the cub thought he was playing games with him! The more he chased him away, the more the bear batted at his legs and followed right behind him.

"Stop! Little Bear! Stop!" Peteetneet said sternly.

Will looked very exasperated. "You gotta help me," he said. "I can't let this bear keep following me! What am I going to do with him?"

Just then Squash Head started to laugh. The more he laughed the tears started coming down his cheeks. Will and Peteetneet stared at him in surprise. It was so unlike the older boy. But laughter is contagious, and before long Will started to giggle and then all three were laughing. Ater a few minutes, each lay on the ground exhausted.

"I know you two think it's funny, but tell me, just what am I supposed to do with this bear?" Will asked. He looked at the other two expectantly

"Little cub like you," said Squash Head with a big grin on his face, "He think you his new mother."

"Ah, cut it out," Will said wondering if Squash Head was serious.

"We find Grandfather," said Peteetneet, "he know what to do."

Will threw his hands up in the air. "Okay, I give up," he said and started walking down the game trail, the little cub close on his heels.

Peteetneet couldn't keep up. "Must stop," he called and the others realized they all needed some rest. Will sat down. "Let's sit by these trees and see if we can't get a few minutes of sleep," he said.

They all tried their best to get comfortable. Boy, would I like my sleeping roll right now, Will thought. But sleep was a more powerful pull than comfort. His eyelids drooped. "Just an hour," he murmured to himself.

The sun started to peek over the treetops. Its golden shafts of light jerked Will wide awake. He shook the cobwebs out of his head and tried to orient himself.

The excitement of discovering the little bear and the struggles of the day before had made the boys very tired. Even though it was urgent for them to find Grandfather, they were all exhausted after their ordeal with Cub Bear Butler and realized they had to get some rest. If not, they may not be able to help the medicine man when they did find him.

It had been late when they stopped, and now it was long past the time when they wanted to get going. Will and Squash Head helped Peteetneet stand up and position his crutch. The morning sun felt warm on their faces and helped to wash away the dark fears of the day before. It was slow traveling with Peteetneet's injury, but they kept moving and their determination soon paid off.

"Should be close," Peteetneet said.

"Look! I think the clearing where Cub Bear captured us is right up around that bend," Will said excitedly.

"Yes," said Peteetneet, "bushes broken and much trail sign of big struggle."

Suddenly, a small dog came exploding out of the bushes next to the boys.

"Tag!" Will called joyfully. "You're all right!" His dog did a flying leap right into Will's arms and licked him all over his face and neck.

"Whoa! Slow down, boy!" Will said, pleased at the puppy's excitement. Just then Tag noticed the little cub and jumped out of Will's arms. He ran over and greeted the bear with the same enthusiasm he had greeted Will.

Squash Head started to run, and Will had to force himself to stay back with Peteetneet. Soon, they turned the bend and saw the small clearing where they had been captured by the trapper. Will shuddered at the memory.

"There he is, Pete!" He pointed to the other side of the clearing. Squash Head was over by a large pine tree and kneeling down in front of his grandfather. Yellow Jacket was sitting on the ground and leaning against the tree.

As the boys got closer they noticed that Grandfather's face was a sickly gray color. His eyes were closed. He looked very fragile and was not moving.

"*To e ah ruve* (It is all right now)," Peteetneet whispered in his Ute tongue. Will looked at his friend and saw the sorrow etched on his face.

Please don't be dead, Will pleaded to himself.

Next to the old man a small, smokeless fire was burning. Squash Head turned around when the other two boys reached them.

"Grandfather not well but alive," he said softly.

"Grandfather! Can you hear me?" Peteetneet whispered, *"oom mah p cuckie* (are you in pain)?"

The man stirred and reluctantly opened his eyes. His lips quivered and a small smile appeared on the weathered old face.

"Now Grandfather happy," he whispered, "can go in peace."

CHAPTER 29

The Magic of The Bear

All three boys stared at Grandfather. They were speechless. "What do you mean, 'go in peace'?" Peteetneet asked him. The old man looked kindly into the eyes of his grandson.

"Grandfather proud of boys," he said as he turned and looked intently at the necklace around Squash Head's neck. "You have done work of warrior, and from this day you be one." He paused a moment, struggling to get his breath. "Give me the telling so I can go to meet my sons," he said weakly.

The boys were very solemn and looked each other. Who should speak? Slowly, Peteetneet began to tell Grandfather what happened after the trapper forced them to leave the clearing early the day before.

Was it only a day ago? Will thought to himself. Squash Head and then Will added their parts to the adventure. Grandfather looked at each one when they were speaking. His eyes widened in amazement as he listened to how narrowly the boys had escaped from the evil man.

"We don't know if he died," Will said at the end of the story. "He was definitely unconscious when we left the cabin, but neither of us wanted to stay around to find out his condition."

"Not worry," Grandfather whispered, "Great Spirit watched over you and spared your lives. The trapper was cruel to the family of Mother Earth. We let Great Spirit take care of fate of white man."

Will looked at the other two boys. He wasn't about to say anything, but he sure hoped the trapper wasn't going to be around to hurt any more bears, let alone people.

"Now is time for Yellow Jacket to *pike-way*," Grandfather said. "We have finished what needed to be done." His old eyes then looked up at Will. "I did not know why you were to go on this journey, but again I have learned why one never question wisdom of Great Spirit."

"Grandfather, must you go?" Peteetneet said sadly.

"It is time. I am very old and must move on. You must free the spirits of my sons and your fathers. Do not be sad. I follow them. Together we wait for day when you too join us in Happy Hunting grounds."

Grandfather held out his hands so the boys could lift him up to sit a little taller. He felt as light as a little child. When he was sitting more comfortably, he slowly reached for one of the pouches at his side, opened it

151

and took out a small packet of dried roots and leaves.

"These are sacred plants you must scatter over clearing. It cleanse the ground and allow our spirits to leave this place where much evil has been done. Peteetneet, it is your duty to do this. You have been taught the way."

He looked at the boys, as though waiting for their consent. Even though there was no question about them doing as the old man asked, their faces were full of the grief they felt in their hearts.

Will looked at the others. He still had a question he wanted to ask. He understood why Grandfather wanted Squash Head and Peteetneet to come on the journey. It ended the mystery of where their fathers had disappeared to. But why had he been invited?

"Grandfather," Will said, "I am honored that you asked me to come on this journey, but I still don't understand why."

Yellow Jacket smiled weakly at Will. "During planting moon, when white boy escaped anger of mother bear, it was sign that magic of bear would follow you. You know from sacred bear ceremony that bears watch out for Blue Sky people. Many time they teach our people lessons we need. Sometime lessons come in strange way."

Will looked into Grandfather's eyes but was still puzzled. He just didn't quite understand what the medicine man was trying to tell him.

"I threw the bones to see your fate but only see this journey. It made clear to me now.

"At the cabin, she-bear sensed your kindness. She

knew you trying to save cub. This kindness also touch Squash Head. He forgot hatred of white man when you bravely follow him back into cabin. He understand all white men not bad. The magic, Little Bear, is your friendship.

"When man forget himself to help another man, this is magic. Bear sent you to help us heal our hurting hearts and remind us to pass on gift of friendship. The white man is now part of our land. No more will Indian roam these mountains alone. We must learn to trust each other."

"Now, Little Bear, cub your responsibility. You protect him until he join his own kind."

Grandfather had spoken too long. He slumped back, exhausted from the effort.

"When will that be?" Will asked quietly.

"When time comes, you know."

Finished speaking, Grandfather leaned heavily against the trunk of the big tree. A great weariness came over the old man's body. The corners of Yellow Jacket's mouth turned up and he formed a weak smile. He gazed for a moment into the eyes of each of the boys. Will could see a glint of satisfaction shine in the tired old eyes and watched as the medicine man released a deep sigh. Yellow Jacket's eyelids slowly closed. Frozen, the boys watched in silence as Grandfather took one last deep breath. He slowly exhaled and with this gentle expulsion of air, it seemed to them that Grandfather's spirit did leave his tired old body and was set free.

CHAPTER 30

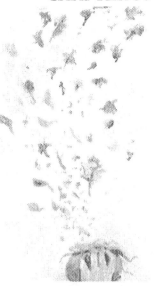

Spirits Free
and
Will's Destiny!

Peteetneet raised his arms high, fingers reaching up as though to touch the very clouds. His head was flung back, long black hair flowing loosely in a gentle breeze, eyes closed tightly, a single tear escaping out of the corner of one eye. The words of his prayer were directed to the heavens above.

Will sat at the edge of the clearing and watched reverently as Peteetneet performed this part of the sacred burial ceremony.

Oh Wind,
I feel your gentle breath
brush kisses
through my hair.
Your brother rain
fills my eyes
to overflowing.
Little rivers
fall over the smooth places
of my face.

Oh wind,
your father,
the Great Spirit,
has taken my grandfather
to soar
as the eagle
among the clouds.

He searches for
his sons,
Wa-Yo-Shaw and Standing
Bear.

Oh wind,
blow your mighty breath.
Send his spirit
quickly
to the high places.

And at the top
let him
embrace his sons.
Together they will soar
forever
as specks of dust
or gusts of wind
never
to part again.

Oh wind,
take him from us
on your strong arms,
free to go
forever more.

The burial would not be completed until they put Grandfather's body in the rock crevice Squash Head had found and then sealed it with stones and mud to keep it safe from wild animals. But first, in order to complete the wishes of Yellow Jacket, they had to cleanse the ground so the spirits of him and his sons could leave and roam forever free.

Squash Head held Peteetneet's walking stick, and when his cousin lowered his arms he motioned for Will to come and help.

Will walked over to the two boys and took the stick from Squash Head. He knew Squash Head was honoring him by allowing him to participate.

Peteetneet solemnly took the packet of dried plants that Grandfather had given him from the pouch at his own waistband. Will and Squash Head stepped back as Peteetneet opened the packet and, raising it high in the air, began chanting softly and sprinkling the contents into the air. As if from nowhere, the breeze suddenly turned into a whirlwind and picked up the special herbs. Astonished, Will watched as they began twisting and turning in a tight circle. The wind increased and the circle grew larger and larger. Will's hair blew in his face, and he impatiently brushed it back out of his eyes.

What's happening here, he wondered.

As he watched, the circle continued to grow and, the bits of leaves and plants twirled faster and faster. The wind became so noisy Will could no longer hear the birds chirping or, for that matter, any other noises of the forest.

"What is this?" he yelled out to Peteetneet and Squash Head. But his voice became lost in the sucking noise of the wind as it reached higher in the sky.

All three boys watched the funnel grow until it filled the little clearing. The leaves and sticks whirled faster and faster until suddenly, the funnel swooped upward in the sky until it was no longer visible. The wind immediately stopped, and again there was only a gentle breeze ruffling the leaves on the quaky trees. The noises of the forest returned, and Will noticed again the songs of the birds calling each other—just as though nothing had happened. He was speechless. He didn't know what to say, even if he could speak. He had never witnessed anything like this in his life.

For the second time, Peteetneet dropped his hands to his sides. He looked bone tired. Squash Head reached out to Will for the walking stick. He handed it to him and watched while Squash Head helped Peteetneet adjust it under his arm and then hobble over to a nearby rock where he sat down. Besides being tired, he looked sad. Will didn't know what to do or say, so he just stood there.

Soon Peteetneet looked up at Will. "Many thanks, my friend," he said with a small smile. "The spirits of our fathers and grandfather are now gone. They are free, and this land is clean."

Squash Head added, "We now take Grandfather's body and put it to rest in arms of Mother Earth." He motioned for Will to follow him.

Will walked over to Yellow Jacket's body and looked at him. Sadly he remembered how the medicine man had closed his eyes after talking to the boys. He never opened them again. When the boys realized he was gone, they took Will's wool blankets and tightly covered and wrapped the body. It was ready now to be laid to rest.

"Come, we make travois to carry body," he said to Will and with his knife began whacking off a few stout branches from the surrounding trees. Will didn't have a knife anymore after their encounter with Cub Bear, so he took the branches Squash Head cut and began stripping off the leaves and small twigs, making them smooth to the touch.

Soon there was a small pile of clean, straight sticks. They took two of the sticks that were about six feet long and laid them horizontally next to each other on the ground. Next they cut up more of the sticks into two foot long pieces. They took the small sticks and laid them between the two long sticks. Taking small strips of leather from their pouches, they tied the small sticks onto the long ones. They now had a frame to put the body on. They would be able to drag the travois with the body on it to the rocks. With Peteetneet's injury it would have been too hard to try and carry the body and the rest of their gear.

Squash Head lifted Grandfather's fragile body and gently put it on the frame. Fortunately, when the trapper had forced the boys to follow him to his cabin, he had not bothered taking their cooking and camping items with him. They could now load these on the travois with Grandfather. They knew they still had a two-day journey to make it back home, and these supplies would make it much easier to get back.

"Are you okay walking?" Will asked Peteetneet as he lifted the other stick on the front of the travois to help Squash Head pull it.

"I have easy part," Peteetneet said with an attempt at light-heartedness, "you pull and me leave both of you behind!"

"Just try it!" Will said, equally trying to change the mood of the group.

The boys started out. Pulling the makeshift rig was

not as easy as it looked. Half the time one of the legs would fall in a gopher hole or get caught on a root.

Eventually they made it to the place where they wanted to bury Grandfather. Earlier, Squash Head had gone back to the river. There was a large, rock-strewn sloping hill that led down to the river bed, and he had hoped to find a safe place for the body on that hill. It hadn't taken him long to find just the right spot. There was a crevice between three big granite boulders that came together and made a small tight-fitting cave. It was situated high above any danger of flooding waters from the river. A perfect place to protect Grandfather's remains.

"Careful," Will yelled as he started down the side of the hill. His feet were slipping in loose gravel, and he was losing control of his end of the travois. Squash Head stopped for Will to get his balance back.

"We go slow now," he said, "cave right below us."

They only had to go about fifty feet and soon reached the opening of the crevice.

The boys anchored the travois between some rocks. They took the camping gear off and carefully untied the straps holding the medicine man's body.

"Help pick up Grandfather and slide him into rocks," said Squash Head.

Will picked up the old man's feet and held him up while the older boy carefully guided the body into the opening of the rock cave.

Soon they had Grandfather in his final resting place. Both boys knew they were performing a sacred duty and were very sober as they completed this task.

"Hand me his belongings," Squash Head said to Will. Will handed him Grandfather's eating cup, his pouches and hunting tools. He wished they could use these things to help them get home, but he knew the others wouldn't even consider it. When a man died, his belongings were buried with him. He would need them for his journey to the Happy Hunting Grounds.

After carefully placing the items Grandfather would need for this last journey, Squash Head squeezed his own body out of the skinny opening in the cave.

All three boys stood and looked at the cave. It was a quiet moment and each were lost in their own memories of the strong man that laid silently before them.

Squash Head, being the practical one of the group said, "We get mud at river and close up opening. Then Grandfather be safe."

The mud on the banks of the river was of a perfect consistency for what they needed. It was a heavy, gray clay material. It would bake hard in the hot summer days and keep all intruders away from the body. Again, the Great Spirit seemed to be helping them.

Once the boys started hauling the clay-like mud up to the cave site, Will realized that physically, the hardest part was yet to come. Sealing off the entrance with small rocks and this sticky clay was not going to be an easy task!

"Are you sure we have to finish this right now?" Will asked while looking at the river and thinking how nice a dip in the cool waters would feel.

Peteetneet looked at Will. There was not even a twinge of a smile on his face.

"Must get Grandfather in resting place quickly," he said, "do not want to anger the spirits."

Will looked at his friend and, when he saw how serious he was, realized that death and burial were not something the Indians wanted to drag out. It was a responsibility to be completed as soon as possible. They were much more superstitious than Will's people. But, that was okay. By now he had learned there were a lot of differences between each of their peoples. Rather than worry about those differences, he would accept them and just hope they would accept his differences. Besides, he had never had a better friend than Peteetneet in his life, so what did it matter?

It took the rest of the day and well into the evening before they filled the last little crack in the cave opening.

"That will do," Squash Head said slapping the excess mud off of his hands and observing their work.

"Yes, Grandfather now go in peace," said Peteetneet. "We mourn with our village when we return."

Will looked at the two Ute-ahs and when he was sure they were finished he said, "Yeah, and now here I go in the river!" With that, he ran down the hill and jumped into the clean and cool water. It felt so good to wash all the sticky mud and dirt off. More than that, as he dunked his head under the water, he felt as though he were washing away the dirt and memory of mean old Cub Bear Butler.

The other two boys started to laugh. Squash Head let loose with a loud whoop and ran down the hill to join Will. With a big smile, Peteetneet slowly hobbled down after them. He reached the edge of the water and rinsed his hands and face as best he could. Will pulled himself onto a rock next to Pete and tried to help him. When they were finished the three boys lay on some boulders, closed their eyes and let the gentle evening breeze warm and dry them.

"We camp here for night," Peteetneet said to them, "start journey back home when sun rises."

"Boy, have we got a telling for your people!" Will said.

Squash Head sat fingering the sacred necklace around his neck. A faraway look came into his eyes. He looked down river where the little white cub and Tag were playing by the water. He then looked at Will and spoke.

"Bear is sacred to our people. Grandfather right when he say bear give you magic. Bear part of your destiny. Squash Head hope Little Bear be his friend."

Will blushed. "Ah shucks," he said, "no hard feelings." Nothing else needed to be said.

"Boy, wait till my ma and pa see this little white bear cub!" he said, changing the subject and suddenly realizing he would soon have another big obstacle to overcome. Little did he know that this was just the beginning of numerous obstacles and adventures that would change the way he thought about many things in his life.

Little could he know that the Blue Sky people, rulers of the Shining Mountains, would tell this story for generations to come.

ENDNOTES

"The Utes are typical Indians. There is probably not a purer type of American Indian. They are virtuous, honest and free from licentiousness; they are humane and kind to one another. They love their children and never abuse them by punishing them as white people do. If they seem to us a peculiar people, they can nevertheless teach us many a lesson in keeping promises."
(George A. Smith, Utah Indian Service)

The real Chief Peteetneet, not entirely trusting the whites, is known to have remarked, "What the white man say go in one ear and out the other, but what Brigham (Young) says goes to the heart and stays there."

Because he was so helpful to the pioneers, a school was built in his honor in 1901 called "The Peteetneet School" in Payson, Utah. It is now a town museum.

The Deseret News of Salt Lake City, Utah gave notice of Chief Peteetneet's death, announced as follows:
"Chief Peteetneet, famous Ute Indian, passed away December 23, 1861 near Fort Crittenden west of Lehi."

Chief Squash Head was known for good and bad in the history of Central Utah, but mainly for the atrocities he committed against the whites. However, some good has been found in his character, for in 1978 the city of Santaquin, Utah, named a small park in his honor.

Madoline C. Dixon; *These Were The Utes*, (Provo, Utah: Press Publishing Limited, 1983, 1994)

For information on where to purchase or
how to order additional copies of this book,
please write:

Grandma Chubby's Books
P.O. Box 902308
Sandy, Utah 84092
lenore@ashbyfamily.com

or contact
Granite Publishing and Distribution
(800) 574-5779 · (801) 229 9023